THE GRID SERIES

BOOK THREE

BOUNCE

JAS T. WARD

To the fans- This is the world you demanded.
Thank you so much for inspiring me to create it.

THE GRID SERIES READING ORDER:

Candyman: Book One
Madness: Book Two
Bounce: Book Three
Lust: Book Four
Cowboy: Book Five
Murder: Book Six
A Mark and a Bite – Website Exclusive Short
Envy: Book Seven
Hostage: Grid Spin-Off – K. Bromberg's Worlds
Chaos: Book Eight
Sundown: Final

INTRODUCTION

Wisdom says that one's past makes one's future. Both intertwine with the present to weave the cloth of one's life in a tapestry of events that show the whole play of time.

But what happens when a past is forgotten.

The threads of memory hidden away to prevent the cloth of time from being unfolded as to prevent it from being ripped apart at the seams?

Power can destroy. Power can create. But when powers with no known purpose are pushed too far, can a love for mankind save it?

This is the story of Bounce.

The god without a past. The god with an unspoken and unknown future. And a god with a destiny and the power to save us all.

Shame he can't remember that.

But someone does.

CHAPTER ONE

Eons Ago

He was sick of pineapple. Coconuts too, so as the smell of roasted wild boar on the tropical island breeze hit his senses, his mouth watered and he followed the scent. Leaving behind his large thatched hut as he wrapped only a colorful dyed cloth around his naked hips, he walked the long winding path through the jungle to get to the main village.

He completely ignored the villagers as they fell to their knees in worship as he passed; the looks from doe- eyed native girls as they swooned with just a glance along with the heated looks of jealously from their mates who were afraid to confront.

No, his mind was completely focused on getting to the central fire pit for a juicy portion of that delicious meat.

Walking up to find the leader of the village had also fallen to his knees, he placed a hand on the gentle older man's shoulder man to murmur, "Stop that. It is not what I wish."

The man rose to give him a smile. "Yes I know, Malihini, but it shows respect. A god should demand respect."

He smiled at the elder's wisdom and the name they had given him. It meant 'visitor' which had nothing to do with his name at all. For he was without a name.

Neither he nor the good people of this island knew what name he was given at birth. Or that he was even born. They just knew he was a visitor that appeared as if dead one day on their beach. Pale and water-logged as if drown in the crystal blue waters that surrounded the island. Bare of clothes or anything—except for healed scars on his shoulders—they had carried him to their village to prepare for a lost soul burial; which didn't happen when he woke up the next morning as alive as they were. Needless to say, that event and those that followed would have them believing he was a god. And he had nothing to debate that fact.

Malihini had no memories. Not a single one of how he got to that beach. What landed him on that island or anything that had happened before. He had no past that he could recall and had no idea if he was missed or fed to the sea to make gone from someone's life. No childhood whispers of parents or siblings. Nothing. His mind was a clean slate without a single recall of events prior to waking up in this village.

That had been more than two years ago and he had been well taken care of. Too much so. He chaffed at their worship and constant striving to please him. All he wanted was to sit on the beach, look at the water and try to dig through an empty mind to find something that would give him a clue as to who or what he was. The villagers would bring him food several times a day to the elaborate hut they had built for him on the farthest side of the isolated island. They provided the wraps he wore to cover himself as well as all the things that adorned his home. And now apparently, they wanted to offer more.

"The elders and I have met Malihini. I wish to

discuss with you." The chieftain, who was called Ali'I, had an almost sheepish smile which caused Mali to pause in chewing the succulent pig, still hot from the fire-spit as he chewed it.

His brow went up in puzzlement as he regarded Ali'I. "With me? I do not wish to be involved with village affairs." He ripped off another hunk of meat from the pig's haunches. "We have discussed that before hoaloha."

Ali smiled as he nodded, "Yes Mali but this concerns you. We need to talk." He turned and walked towards his hut. Though the man was the chief, his hut was half the size of Mali's. But unlike his, the chief's hut was full of five wives. Two of which were round with child as the other herded the chief's eleven children of various ages and sizes.

Mali loved going inside to be wrapped up in the warmth, laughter and chaos of the leader's family. The women were completely one with nature with dark tanned skin, beautiful black hair though some streaked with grey and wore only the native colorful wraps around their bosoms. They all giggled and whispered behind their hands as he entered with the chieftain and he gave them a smile causing them to whisper louder and wave their wraps slowly in a discreet show of flesh and curves.

It amused Mali, as he had seen the entire village nude. Living on a tropical island, clothing was not a required item when living with nature. The women and men of the village were all beautiful in their own way and Mali loved the lack of false modesty and useless vanity among the people.

They swam nude, ran and played in the nude with no inhibitions that their bodies were anything to be hidden or be ashamed of. Only mated and married women wore the beautifully dyed cloths to hide their fertile curves from others eyes. Their husbands did the same out of respect for their wives.

Mali did it to prevent the constant wave of desire from women and jealously from men. He stood out from the people as most of them averaged five feet, six inches tall and he stood far above at six foot eight. Their skin was dark from being raised under the sun and while his also was sun-kissed, it had an olive complexion with black hair and his face displayed more refined features. He knew his body was one which was wanted by the females of the island. Chiseled muscle that ripped down his torso, leading to long and strong legs all made him stand out among the lean people. He wasn't deaf to the giggles and laughter of the women, young and old, that spied from the brush as he swam in the nude on his side of the island. It amused him a great deal.

But it was his eyes that would cause none to doubt that he was not a human as such as those around him.

His eyes were an ever-changing color depending on his moods. From pure ocean blue to a deep red all indicating what thoughts were running through Mali's head. Whatever emotion was riding reign could be told by the hue of his eyes. Red rarely showed. So much so that only he had seen it in fits of frustration and rage when he was alone at the fact of having no memory. He hid that side from the good people of the village for it had come with a show of powers that had scared even he. It would have horrified the kind villagers. And he wished no harm to them. Or anyone.

Sitting by the fire across from the chief on one of the palm tree stumps used for stools, he licked his fingers and waited for the man to tell him how anything in governing the village concerned him.

"We want to give you wives."

Mali stopped licking pig juices from his fingers, frozen in place by the chief's words. The women all hushed as well to listen to the conversation like gossipy hens. Fixating his eyes on the pad of his thumb, Mali's dark brows came down as if there was some sudden defect in the digit.

He knew the villagers wanted him here. He also knew the chief was smart in that as well. What other neighboring tribe would attack an island that housed a god? One whose powers were unknown and therefore feared? It didn't matter that he had never shown one aggressive bone or mean nature as he never felt the need or want to do so. He himself didn't understand his powers, so he let them lie untouched except when they flared unexpectedly. Like when the village was overtaken by some plague from bacteria that had struck the fish last summer. He had been able to heal with just a touch and wish in his head to help the suffering people. They had healed by morning. He had no idea how he was able to do that. Just that he did.

Dropping his hand, he lifted his gaze to the chief's to see how serious the man was or if this was, as he hoped, a joke. "Wives? As in females? To mate?"

The chief nodded and then cleared his throat. "Unless it is males you seek? It is not our nature, but we only wish to make you happy."

The females' eyes went wide as if that thought had not occurred to them and Mali raised a hand up quickly to dispel that idea, "No. I do not seek males. I desire females." The chief started to speak again to make it so, but he cut him off fast. "But I do not wish you to give me wives. Or a wife. Or a female at all. It's not what I want. You don't have to do that."

He was assuming this was yet another ploy to get him to stay. To tie Mali to the village in order to continue to be a deterrent from attack from other tribes.

Of course Mali had desires for companionship. For the warm curves of a woman and soft whispered sighs of pleasure in the night sea breeze, but it had to do with his lost past.

What if he had a woman? A wife? Children? All wondering when the one they loved would return. Add to that he sought more than just rutting and sweating. He had nothing in his head and nothing in his heart. It was all an empty space. He wanted to fill it with more than lust and desire.

He wanted love.

The chief stood and clapped his hands. The flap by the hut entrance was opened and more than a dozen beautiful island girls rushed in. They immediately dropped their cloths to show their bodies before his eyes. Large breasts, small breasts atop slender waists and rounded ones. Short and tall with teasing dark curls between lovely brown thighs. They all wore flowers in their hair, with some having taken the time to weave blossoms into necklaces or bracelets. Some were barely out of puberty while others were well past it. But all of them were the most beautiful unmated women on the island.

Mali dropped his chin to his chest to hide the amused smile as well as the hint of blush on his cheeks. The women all sighed in adoration and he shook his head slowly to say, "I appreciate your offer. But I do not seek to be given anything. Your people have given me a home. Food and shelter. It is I that owe you." He stood and one of the women, bolder than the rest walked up to stand in front of him.

He looked down and let his eyes wander without command down her body and back up. She was young yet a woman with the typical village dark skin and hair. Her eyes were a lovely greenish-brown with full lips and perky nose. Her breasts were ripe and full and even as he looked, she brought a hand up to make one swell to a rosy tip. She placed a hand on his chest, her fingers stroking and said softly with a seductive tone, "I can please you Malihini. I am not new to the ways of making a man want. You can pay your debt for my people's kindness with me."

He smiled and gently removed her hand from his chest. He did not wish to hurt the woman's feelings and his body showed her very easily under his light cloth how much he believed her statement in the fact it he had a pointer right in her direction. She smiled as she brought that hand down, with his hand still wrapped around her wrist, to brush over it under the soft material and he sucked in a breath.

"You are lovely. But as I said—I do not wish a mate. Or a wife. Or," looking up to see the other women who were trying to get his attention from the one that was being so friendly, "wives. Mahalo."

He stepped away from the wanton female to give the chief a nod as he made his way to the door, bracing his hand on his aching erection to make it behave as he reentered the sunlight. The women all followed as well as the chief's wives and the chief himself all chattering and begging him to listen.

"Mali. Have we offended you? If so, did so only out of ha'aha'a. Nothing more." "Please do not leave us!"

He sighed and turned to face them and smiled. "No. It is fine. I do feel honored that you have offered such a gracious gift. But", he looked at them all, "I'm not ready. But no worries, I have nowhere else I need to go. My word on that will have to do."

He then turned and left them there.

He was going to need a swim. Why did the ocean have to be so warm? Ice cold was what he needed to chill some heated parts.

Before he stabbed a tree with it.

CHAPTER TWO

Fate and Sand

Lachesis just wanted to hide, to take some time away from her family and her duties if only for a week. To be somewhere foreign and tropical with warm breezes, white sand and blue oceans and it not be Greece. So, as she gave that thought power, she was pleased to find herself on a remote island in the middle of a blue sea.

Bending down to remove her leather sandals, she sighed in pleasure as she wiggled her toes in the sun heated sand and closed her eyes in the salt and flowered scent air. This was paradise. Sure, Mount Olympus, the kingdom of the Greek gods, was beautiful. But sometimes, Lachesis, thought it was a façade for the darkness of the beings it contained. Jealous and greedy, selfish and self-centered gods and goddesses that had so much power yet did very little good with it.

As a goddess of fate, it was Lachesis and her two sisters'—Clotho and Atropos duty to maintain the destinies of every single living being on the human realm. It was not an easy job and the stress of it took its toll on the goddesses.

But unlike her sisters who would use the distractions of Mount Olympus with its ambrosia and well trained servants to meet all their needs, Lachesis liked coming to the human realm. Her family of deities gave her hell about wallowing in the squalor of mankind when the greatest of all pleasures could be found on high but she didn't care. She loved coming below among the humans with their wonderful hearts and cherishing in a life that was not immortal. It humbled her and it was also an escape. One that she wished she could take more often.

Mali was sitting in the warm sand after a long swim to watch the tide roll in under the bright sun above. He loved watching the receding and the approaching water and never missed a tide. Whereas low tide would sometimes bring treasures in the form of shells, driftwood and other things, it sometimes brought him things from faraway lands. He always wondered if it was land he was from or if it would just take one touched piece from another shore to bring back his memories.

However, in the two years of doing this, the watery giver of gifts had never given what he once was—a person from its depths. He often wondered if he offered himself back to the tide if it would carry him back to where ever it was he had come.

He was entertaining that thought when a movement down the shoreline caught his attention. Looking sideways, he got a puzzled look as he saw what appeared to be a woman walking along the foam of the approaching surf. She wore some sort of wrap of white, but it covered her from shoulders to bare feet on one shoulder held in place by a golden belt at the waist and a brooch at the collarbone. She held leather strapped sandals dangling from her fingers in one hand while the other hand held one of the island's native flowers of dark pink spinning in her fingertips in the other. Her hair was the most beautiful of chestnut brown which contrasted deliciously against pale, creamy skin. He had never seen a woman so unearthly beautiful, well, that he could remember. Which wasn't saying too much considering. But she could never be mistaken as a villager for she was too perfect and aloof and definitely not a carefree island dweller.

Getting to his feet, with sand the only thing on his skin, he stood and tilted his head as she made her way towards him. He didn't think she saw him and that fact was confirmed when she stopped, stiffened and then blushed at his nudity. That made him smile and he tilted his head the other way in amusement.

Lachesis had known there were residents on the island. But she had made sure to manifest her form on the far side from them. To see a totally nude man with the body that would have any god envious and any goddess wanting to worship it standing before her was a shock. But not because he was there. But because of the power that she sensed off him in waves. A god? Here?

Why had she not picked up on that? She should have sensed him before she even appeared here, as the fates were some of the strongest gods among her pantheon.

Those thoughts vanished as she took in his appearance, telling herself it was to figure out what kind of god he was—but knowing it was because the man was absolutely beautiful. Tawny olive skin, muscles that were cut as if in marble and as Lachesis let her eyes trail down a dusting of dark hair on his flat, ripped stomach, impressive in all the ways that mattered.

No one was more surprised by her blush than she was, but then when she saw the man's amusement it only worsened and she felt even more embarrassed.

She considered vanishing to deal with her humiliation. Why would a man just stand there? Totally nude? Totally delicious with sand dusting his skin like sugar that made her want to lick the skin underneath.

Lacy! She chastised herself as she straightened her spine in a dignified goddess way that would have made her step-mother, the wife of Zeus proud.

"Greetings" She used her most dignified voice as she ran her hands down her robe, realizing she still held the flower and dropped it. Along with her sandals with a clumsy sounding thud. Pride from her family would have vanished at that moment.

The man gave a wider smile in a face that would have made master artists cry with its perfection in efforts to capture it on canvas it as he stepped up and knelt down to pick up her sandals. Lachesis commanded her eyes go upward as she got a glimpse that the backside was as perfect as the front. She demanded the thoughts of wanting to bite the perfect ass cheek he had as he stood to stop.

"Aloha." Oh of course, she thought, his voice would sound like sex on a song. Deep with an exotic accent that she had never heard...wait. That wasn't possible. As a high goddess, all languages and accents were known by her by nature. How could any being have one she didn't know or recognize?

She narrowed her eyes as she yanked her shoes from his fingers to stare at him. Before her eyes, the color of his went from a deep blue to a crystal lighter shade instantly. She blinked and leaned in to look closer, not even aware she was dangerously close to touching parts that would make the other naughty thoughts in her head look like nursery rhyme musings.

"What are you?" She whispered softly as she waited for his eyes to change.

Mali was so entertained right now. As she scrutinized his face, he couldn't help but do the same. Her skin was flawless and her lips were full even when she twisted them in concentration as if working a puzzle. Her eyes were the most beautiful of brown with a cute nose with a button on the tip. The blush she had worn so delightfully just a few moments ago had left her skin but even so, her cheeks were a faint pink as if she wore some sort of facial paint, but none that he could see. She smelled of something he had never gotten a whiff of before but it pleased him. It was musky and sweet all at the same time as if her skin was washed in it. He couldn't help but wonder what it tasted like.

"I don't know what I am. But I ask the same of you, Nani."

Lachesis blinked at him calling her beautiful in the native tongue. She didn't think anyone had called her that. Ever. Not the other gods or goddess nor the human servants that worshipped the residents of Mount Olympus. The Fates were not known for their beauty and most all feared the power they held with just a snip of shears, a snap of fingers, a lack of caring of a soul thread they held in their hands.

"You think I'm beautiful?"

The man smiled and nodded. "Yes. Why? Don't you?"

Lachesis opened her mouth to speak and all that was uttered was a squeak. No. She did not. Unlike goddesses like Artemis and Aphrodite, she did not spend hours in the mirror admiring her own image or beating slaves for not telling her she was the most beautiful woman in the world after commanding to do so with a look. She had a duty and it was one that took up most of her time. Vanity she had no time for. Crossing her arms and giving him a snobby glare, she said in a voice that would have made even a god shrivel, in retrospect, shrivel was perhaps not the best word, because he wasn't shriveling at all..."Why are you here? And why are you naked?"

Mali cocked an eyebrow up and let his eyes trail down at her strange robe-like dress, "Why are you here? And why are you dressed?"

Lachesis jaw dropped in indignation and she sputtered, yes, she sputtered. A high goddess who made gods quake with one look was sputtering. She was taken aback by his question and pointed at him. "Because being dressed is what decent beings do. It's proper. It's..." she thought about how she sounded and narrowed her eyes in frustration, "it makes for easier conversation without a bunch of," waved her hand at him, "distraction."

Mali smiled wide to reveal perfect white teeth and fangs. Fangs? Was Lachesis actually seeing fangs? She leaned in close to look as he said in that rich with promises voice, "So, does my body distract you?"

If she had thought she blushed before? It was nothing to the heat that blasted through her now. Of course he was distracting, she told herself. With his big body, perfect muscles, beautiful face and angelic features and well, other impressive things. Didn't he know that would distract anything with a pulse? She wasn't dead after all. But considering, maybe even the dead would be finding it hard to breathe and think with a man like this standing there. Like that. Naked. And... Well, did she use impressive already? Because it was getting more impressive by the second.

"Can you not put something away? I mean," she flustered and a deep red piece of woven cotton appeared in her hand, "put something on?" She thrust the material at him and he took it, but with hesitation. He looked at it and then her before wrapping it around his hips. Even that looked sinful, she thought, but at least the most obvious distraction was no longer waving at her.

"Did you? How?" He brushed his hands over the soft material as a frown of bafflement crossed his features, "How did you just make this appear?"

Lachesis stared at him. She had no doubt he was a god. And a powerful one. Other than that she had not a clue. But surely he was not ignorant of the powers of their kind. "Can you not manifest?"

He looked up at her and his bafflement only deepened with a slow shake of his head. "I don't know? I could perhaps. But have never tried? Or needed to."

Lachesis was never more confused or intrigued. As a fate, she knew all beings on earth by a thought. A touch or the moment they spoke. As she pondered the strange man before her, she realized she got nothing from him. Not a hint, not a clue and nothing that told her a single thing about him.

How was that even possible?

She stepped away from him in bafflement and

watched as he felt the cloth like it was magical alone, "You are a god, yes?"

Mali looked up at her and shrugged to say flatly, "That is what they tell me. I know not. But I don't believe I can make such fine things from thin air."

Lachesis was now totally captured in the mystery of this beautiful man in front of her. Stepping up, she met those strange eyes and watched them go from a light blue to a dark forest green. "What's your name?" Fascinating!

The man frowned and lowered his lashes to cover his gaze and said softly, "I do not have a name. They call me visitor," lifting his now dark, stormy grey eyes to hers, "their word for that is Malihini."

Lachesis felt such sadness come off of him in sorrowful waves. He had no idea. No idea about anything that had to do with...him. And she knew she would help him. Somehow.

"My name is Lachesis."

CHAPTER THREE

No History

Lachesis walked around the large hut, brushing her fingers over the beautiful handmade crafts and carvings that sat on shelves and nooks. The interior was simple with a large bed in one corner made of wood with rope and a large mattress stuffed with soft dried sea weed. The sheets were colorful dyed cloth much like the man apparently wore. Over each doorway, the natives had carved symbols of blessing and adoration to the man who lived within. A long porch was on the front of the palm leave thatched hut to look out on the beach. It was truly a temple in paradise. Nothing like the white, cold marble temple as her sisters and she had in Mount Olympus.

"They worship you?" Her eyes went to a wooden tray that was heavily laden with fresh fruit and meat dropped off only moments ago by a beautiful native girl. Lachesis had to stop herself from wondering how many of those native girls this man had laid with in that big soft bed.

Mali came back to lean against doorway across from her, his eyes cast to the sea. "They do. I tell them they do not have to. But they feel I am worthy of worship." He swung his gaze to regard her. "I wish they would not because I do not feel I am."

Lachesis returned his look, searching his eyes, once again fascinated in their changing colors. Now they were as dark brown as if black which showed no emotion but yet seemed so full of it. She just wasn't sure which emotion he was trying to hide.

"It's their nature. Humans worship so that we gods will protect. Make their crops grow. Have healthy babies. A human's need to worship is as strong as it is to breathe." She turned to face him with her hands on the beam behind her. "What do you remember?"

Mali shrugged as he crossed his arms, muscles bulging at just that simple movement, "Waking up. But it was not like sleep. It was more like", he frowned with elegant brows coming down as he struggled for the right words, "being born. A complete awareness of nothing prior. Of only that moment on. Like an infant kept in a dark silent womb yet fully formed. I knew how to speak. Read. I understood these people without even knowing their language. Could speak it too. But no idea why or how."

Lachesis nodded. "It's a deity's gift. We are born with the knowledge of all ages and times. Cultures too. We carry the same fibers of mankind that our parents did. Passed on."

He tilted his head to look at her. "So I have parents? Are you sure?"

Now Lachesis frowned and sighed. "No. I'm not sure. You would have knowledge of them I would think if you had their fibers of memories." Lachesis worried her bottom lip in her teeth, "There's nothing? No dreams? No nightmares? Nothing?" She stepped around him to lightly trail her fingers on the only things that marred his beauty—two brutal yet healed scars that went upward on his shoulder blades. "You have no memory of even these?" She moved back to stand in front of him, watching his face.

He shook his head. "No. They were healed when I arrived here. And I remember nothing. I don't dream and I've never had a nightmare. I simply go to sleep out of boredom. But I've never been tired. Hunger," pointed to the tray of food, "is something I don't feel either. But I eat for pleasure." He smiled at her. "The roast pork is excellent. The pineapple?" he grimaced "Sick of it. But I don't tell them. They are good people. I never wish them sadness or harm."

Lachesis let out a soft laugh and tilted her head. "Have you ever tried to find out where you came from? What or who you are?"

Mali shrugged as he walked over to lay back on the bed, completely unaware of the raw sexually even the simplest of moves brought to the surface. Lachesis wished she was unaware, but as the god stretched like some relaxed big cat, she had to pull her eyes away. It was silly—as she had seen all forms of the human shape clothed and unclothed, but she had never seen a being so sensual without any effort at all. And not even conscious of it.

"How am I to find out? I appeared here nude," looking at her with a smile, "as you found me. I had no marking other than the scars on my back and no memories. No name." He let out a deep laugh as his head dropped back down. "I tried asking a fish. A bird too. They were no help. So I wait and see."

That fact that he didn't seem alarmed or concerned to know his past or identity baffled Lachesis. His power was great—for even now she could feel it. But that was only when she was so near to him, otherwise she had not sensed him before. Was it for protection? Cloaking? And if so, who had taken such measures to insure he wasn't found. And then washed him up here on an island that would not only take care of him, but worship him? It was a mystery that was too good to pass up.

"I can help you. If you want."

Mali sat up to regard her, a strange look on his face as his eyes phased to a soft green. "You would help me? Why?"

Lachesis wasn't sure, but being a goddess of destinies the thought there was a being whose destiny seemed unwritten and unseen by even her—too tempting to pass up. And he was so sweet and unassuming so maybe it was pure selfishness on her part to want to spend more time with him. It was refreshing and it made her smile. "Because everyone deserves to know where they came from. It helps in where one is going. What one is needed to do. I can help you, but we'll need to leave here."

Mali tilted his head with his eyes narrowing as he listened to her. His gaze then shifted to look beyond her at the surf gently brushing along the sand of the beach. The sunlight glinting so pure off the waves with the breezes swaying the palm trees of his cove. It was beautiful here, of that he was sure—but it was also all he knew. Or remembered. To leave here was something he had never given thought to but now that this beautiful newcomer spoke of doing so he felt a combination of emotions—excitement, trepidation and loss.

The people here had been good to him and accepted him. But he was not ignorant to the fact they also felt they needed him for their safety and security. Sighing, he rose to stand and gave her a nod, "I will go. But I need tonight to tell the people here. They have been good to me and deserve to know I am leaving."

CHAPTER FOUR

Stay and Be Worshipped

The goddess had left at sunset, leaving Mali alone with his thoughts—something he was used to once before but now his mind was troubled. The chief had not taken the news of the island's god leaving well. The tribal elders had fallen to their knees and pleaded with him not to go. He could have whatever he wished to stay—all the tribe's virgins, any of the wives, whatever it took. But Mali now wanted what the goddess Lachesis had to offer—his history and his future by learning who he was.

As he lay there on his bed, his eyes were cast outward at the water under the moonlight and he sighed. He had no idea where Lachesis would be taking him—would it be different than here? Would he receive the same welcome and sense of wanting to belong as he did here? Of that, he had no idea but it was a move forward and that was more than he had ever been offered—once again, that he could remember. It would be nice for Mali to never have to think nor say that again. To know his past, whom he had been, what he was meant for and perhaps, insight into his future.

"Mali?"

He rose on his forearms to see Talia, the chieftain's daughter on her knees in the doorway. Her head was down with long dark hair cascading down to hide her. He frowned but before he could speak, she was standing and he saw that she wore nothing more than moonlight on her skin. Nudity was common within the tribe, but for a maiden to come to a man nude meant only one thing.

Mating.

Talia walked over and he was not sure how to respond. She gave him a shy smile as she climbed next to him in bed to lie against him. "Talia? What are you doing?"

She looked up him with eyes the color of dark sand, her lips colored pink by berry juice, "I have been given to you." She walked over and without another word, slid in bed next to him.

"Given? To me?" Talia was the most beautiful of the chief's daughters and would be a prize to any chief or warrior to be made a mate. Mali looked down at her, his brows coming down as she curled up against him, her skin so warm and scented of island flowers and honey—which meant she had partook in the ritual of a bath as that of a maiden on her wedding night. Her hand brushed down his chest to tease her fingers along his hardening length and he still didn't move, unsure what exactly was going on.

She looked up at him with those deep, dark eyes and purred out, "I can feel that I please you, Mali. Let me please you more."

For her to think that an arousal was an indicator of his pleasure, she was sorely incorrect. A breeze at just the right angle seemed to have the same effect on him as he reached down to grasp her wrist and pull her hand away. "Talia. Stop."

She blinked up at him as she laid back to expose all her curves and valleys, her hand now pulling his hand to touch that same skin. "Am I not beautiful? Do I not feel soft and ready?" She pulled his hand down to the apex of her thighs.

Mali was off the bed in seconds, grabbing his cloth to wrap around his waist, once again internally cursing that the cloth did nothing to hide his erection. He ran his hands through his dark hair as he regarded her when she sat up. She took the pose of a chaste maiden, head down with her legs folded under her, hands in her lap. He closed his eyes as she peeked at him from under her curtain of black hair.

"Talia. Why are you here? Did your father send you?" She nodded and he hissed out a breath of frustration through his teeth.

"He said I should please you. In every way. Offer to be your wife and show you why you needed to stay." She said the words softly, as if afraid to anger him—or to fail on her father's orders. To not obey the chief would bring both shame to her and dishonor punishment from the tribe.

The thought that the chief would put his own daughter in such a position as well as be so desperate to keep Mali here caused his anger to bubble up. It not only shrunk his erection, but increased his frustration. "Come with me." He handed her one of his cloths as he held out his hand.

She blinked at him confused as she wrapped the blue dyed cloth around her naked form and took his hand. He led her out of his hut and down the path to her village. She started to protest as they walked towards the chief's hut, pulling on his hand to stop him.

"Mali," she fell to her knees, her voice full of desperation, "please do not reject me. I will be tainted by the gods and my tribe."

He gently pulled her up and met her eyes, brushing her hair from her face. "Not by this god.

And I won't allow anyone to mark you or dishonor you."

Mali made it to the chief's hut and called out to him. He heard whispered and movements behind the cloth over the door, so he knew they did not sleep within. Which meant his coming here must have been considered. But they also must have hoped he wouldn't.

"Ali'I. We need to speak." Talia hid behind him as he called out once more. The door cloth parted and the chief came out, followed by his many wives and children. Ali'l's eyes went to Talia filled with blame and anger before meeting his.

"She failed to please you? Would you like to choose another? Or many others?" The chief was standing tall and proud but his expression betrayed his abandoned hope.

Mali held up his hand and pulled Talia gently in front of him. "No. I do not wish her to please me. It is not her. It is me. And therefore no blame should be placed on her."

Talia walked forward, her head down to join her family, but as soon as she walked past her father, the man backhanded her, knocking her to the dirt in front of the hut. She cried out and cowered, curling up into a ball as she expected more punishment.

Mali moved faster than any could realize to grab the chief by the throat, lift the man off his feet and slam him against the hut's post. The man struggled for a few seconds before he met Mali's furious expression. The god's eyes were swirling red like a stormy sunset and the man trembled with fear, ceasing his flailing.

"Do not strike her. You will not mark her for shame. Nor will you punish her. Do you understand?"

The chief gave him a wide-eyed look as his wives wailed for his released, pleading for Mali to allow the man to live.

He let him go and turned away, frustration swirling with the desperation for them to just try to see why he needed more than all the generosity they had to offer—why it wasn't enough. He looked at the sky as he blew out a long breath, hoping to abate his emotions before speaking. "I have to know who I am. What I am. Do you not understand that?"

He turned and they all shrunk back, cowering as if they feared him like they did the thunder from the mountain above them. That response made Mali feel shame for having caused that in such a good people, but perhaps that rift what was needed to break their adoration. But he felt so guilty that it had to be broken to begin with.

The chief stood and timidly walked to stand in front of him, though still fearful. "Why must you know? What if it is a past you do not want to know? What if it is one that will destroy the man you have become?"

Mali met his eyes as he raised a hand to gently place on the man's shoulders. "Because how can I be anything if I do not know what I am meant to be? I must know. Even if it destroys me."

CHAPTER FIVE

The Mount of the Gods

Mali had never seen such an amazing place. The goddess Lachesis had appeared in his hut and without gathering any of his belongings and only a single glance back, they had vanished from the only place of home he had known—or remembered.

After what seemed like he was falling for the briefest of seconds, they manifested in front a huge marble temple's inner courtyard. It was surrounded by gardens of the sweetest smelling flowers with water seeming to run through it with no fountain head or a destination as if placed there for beauty rather than function. Lachesis had quickly rushed him inside, checking for others as they made their way to her private chambers.

He pulled her up short when they reached the plush adorned rooms to turn her to face him. "Are you ashamed of me? Why go into hiding as soon as we arrived?"

Lachesis was vexing a nail with her teeth when he stopped her to face him—his eyes were a dark grey which matched an expression of trepidation and confusion. She sighed as she shook her head, "No. It's not shame at all. It's more like survival."

Lachesis sat on a bed that hung above the ground as if floating, supported by unseen chains. She looked away from him to cast her eyes to look outside through the rose-tinted glass of the windows. "It's the other gods. Mainly the King of the gods, named Zeus. My father." Her eyes swung back to meet his. "He's very controlling and he and my cousin, Apollo, do not like strangers from other pantheons or realms." She smirked and looked down at her fingers. "You can thank my cousin Artemis for that one. She likes to rotate lovers through her bedroom like pets to grow tired of." She realized she had spoken that out loud and her eyes widened as her cheeks reddened. "Artemis is very," her brow creased searching for the right word to use, "hungry and friendly."

She smirked as she rose to stand in front of him to look up to meet his eyes, saying softly, "I wouldn't want you to come to harm. Or to have to deal. And I will be honest, the wrath of Zeus is not something either one of us want. Understand?"

Actually, he did not. But what did he know of family dynamics? The only one he thought he understood on the island had been greatly skewed in the last few days, so he gave her a nod, "As you wish. This is your home and I will abide by whatever you ask."

"Now you make it sound like I'm the one treating someone like a pet," the goddess grumbled before taking his hand, "come on, and let me show you around." Using her powers, she sensed her two sisters were not on Mount Olympus as she led him from her chamber to the Well of Souls. The chamber was just as ornate in marble as the rest but no other furnishing adored the room. In the center was a well that came to Lachesis' waist in height and almost eight-feet around. She stood by it with him and held her hand over the water, "Think of someone. Anyone and I will tell you where they are. How they are. At this very moment and any moment in the past."

Mali shrugged. "I know no one..." he thought and pointed to the water. "The village. Can it show me the village?"

Lachesis smiled, not surprised that the kindness of the island's people had made such an impact on the god. "Yes. Let me focus."

Lachesis closed her eyes and ran her fingers into the darkness of the water. Water that seemed to be fathoms deep to Mali. But as he watched, tendrils of bright colors seem to swim and float to the surface, as if wishing to caress her hands. They started a strange dance right beneath the surface of the water at the well's edges until they surrounded the depth, framing the center surface. As they circled faster, the water seemed to take an opaque appearance, like that of a mirror and then showed a scene—a scene that seemed to be as if looking on it with his eyes as if was there.

It was the village and the people seemed fine going about their daily tasks. Dusky skinned children laughed and played as their mothers prepared food and mended simple clothes. Even Talia sat among them and he was pleased to see no shaming mark was branded to her face. "Good. I worry about them. Thank you."

His tenderness was odd to her, coming from someone who was also as powerful as she perceived him to be. She wasn't used to such a soft-hearted view of mankind from gods and goddesses. They seemed to be born with that jaded snobbery towards the humans—humans whose worship they relied on just to exist. Deities are narcissistic by nature, but not Mali and that charmed Lachesis. It was so simple despite the complexity of the unknown god. She turned to face him. "This is how I can help you. As a goddess of fate, one of three, I can try to find your thread which will contain everything about you. Who you are, where you came from and your past, as well as a possible future. Is that something you'd like for me to do? I thought maybe..." her voice trailed off softly, "it would be nice to help someone rather than just observe and not be able to."

He tilted his head at her odd tone, finding it strange that to offer such kindness did not seem the normal for her. She seemed so sweet yet giving to him. He tilted her head up to look at him, her eyes deep with thought, her jaw set for a denial she thought he would give, as he whispered, "Are you so unaccustomed to having such chances, Nani? Or are you often rejected for such offers?"

In truth, Lachesis had never made such an offer as it had been preached into her since birth to never interfere or meddle in the affairs of others using her powers. It was her duty to stand by, unbiased and uncaring, as the very fates she and her sister wove played out. Wars had been fought and lost with even the simplest snip of a thread from the golden shears of the three goddesses of fate—if that war was meant to be. The outcome could be seen, but the choices that were made along the way? Not always in the fates hands. Free will always had its play in it all.

As she looked into the ethereal beauty of the man above her, she felt like free will had forgotten Mali. Where had his choices gone? Why wasn't he allowed to even know what had happened or could happen by a simple decision that could have changed his fate—his free will allowed having not a say? She knew that train of thought would take her to what she had to do, "I have never had the chance before," laying her hand over his on her cheek, "but now that I do? Let me."

It was a chance Mali had dreamed of for as long as he had awoken on that beach but he thought about how she had to sneak him into her chambers, checking and fearing for interruptions the entire time. He tilted her chin with his fingertips to gently tilt her eyes back up to his to say softly, "What risk is this to you Nani? With all your power, why have you not had chances before? And why me?"

Lachesis thought about that, her brow creasing with the thought of it. She saw no guile or greed in Mali's face, his eyes going a soft, forest green as they looked into hers. She was about to agree to break every unspoken rule about the fates of destiny's role in existence. To create, to observe and then...to end. But never to interfere. Only to create the threads and then allow it to weave through life as the fabric of time ordained—knowing the end before the beginning was even ordained but not allowed to change the course. Such was the very serious iron-control of free will.

But Mali had none. Not about his past, so Lachesis closed her eyes, finding she relished in the touch of the strange god, and then opened them once more to meet his. "I do this because I care. I'm not even sure why. But you have been wronged in not knowing your past for it forges our future." She stood to place her hands on his chest as her voice went to a whisper, "So I want to help you, perhaps because I want to be a part of your future."

Lachesis had no idea where the words came from—she didn't even think, a habit she had, before saying them. They came from some place that even she was not aware of and while there was a tremor of fear in finding them now, she knew she would not change her mind. Nor would she question it. For once, Lachesis was going to go with the ebb and flow of destiny as a passenger, rather than a bystander. And it was thrilling.

Mali inclined his head to the side with a soft smile, before saying softly, "I think I would like that. However Nani, there is something I must say," he cupped her face with his hand, "if we find that I have a love in my past, children even, then I must follow see what was meant for my heart with them. If there is a path that can be taken. Does that cease your desire to help me?"

Desire—even the word on his lips, said in that smooth, exotic voice, made Lachesis feel strange. Wanton and liquid as if from a heat from within. But then the words that preceded it dampened that sensation and gave her an abrupt pause. What if he did have a beautiful goddess and children lamenting daily for the one they loved? What if all she was doing was helping him find a lost love and all she would be left with was heartache? For the first time in Lachesis existence the answer was a resounding—yes.

She met his eyes and gave a smile, her doubts vanishing as she did. "Yes. This is about you. Not me. And we'll deal with that when we learn it."

Mali gave her the most dazzling smile as he all but bounced on his feet in excitement. "Then how do we begin? I want to start now."

Lachesis laughed at his infectious excitement as she took his hand. "First, we must see if the pool can show us anything. That is the simplest of ways. If that does not work, I will have to tax my powers to their maximum as I have never not been able to sense someone's thread before," she squeezed his hand tight in her own, "but we will find what we seek. Of that I am sure."

CHAPTER SIX

Frustration

That had been over a week ago and Lachesis was not sure why her powers were failing her, for she was able to find nothing regarding Mali. In fact, no past nor a present. And most definitely not a trace of his future. She had considered more than once asking one of her sisters to assist, but that would mean revealing the god was staying here—forbidden and very likely would be whispered in Zeus' ears by Atropos, Clotho or one of their slaves. No, she had to do this alone and it was wearing her very thin.

She was exhausted having slept very little in the week not to mention not eating. Sure, fatigue and starvation couldn't kill a higher deity such as she, but that didn't mean she didn't feel the effects of it. But it was the helpless frustration that was grinding on her most of all. She had all but promised Mali that she would solve the mystery that was the god, but had nothing to make that commitment a complete and Lachesis was not one used to failure—even if this was the first true challenge she had taken on.

Perhaps that was part of the reason for the frustration. The fact that for once, she had decided to go against how she had also lived and function and the first time she had done so it was a failure.

Mali had been here a week and although she enjoyed his company for he was so pleasant to be around, she was worried that her keeping him secreted here would be discovered and come to a very disastrous end. She had her various god and goddess cousins to thank for that. They were all supposed to be pure and the epitome of behavior, or so Zeus wished. But the gods had an appetite for a wide range of tastes and perversions so Zeus rarely got what he desired in that, but the gods made sure to get whatever they desired without a thought to the king of the gods. Some did it just to spite him, which was never wise. So Zeus had been fiercely over lording who came and went from Mount Olympus. If not a resident, all gods and other higher beings were to be brought in front of the god himself upon stepping foot on the realm to seek permission to be here. Very few honored that rule either, for their visitors were more a use and toss variety rather than representatives of esteem or decorum. Then there was the fact that Zeus had his own appetites and had no qualms in taking some treat from another that he desired himself.

Lachesis only hoped that the distaste and respectful that she and her sisters had among the gods would keep them away, as it usually did, from the Temple of the Souls. Each sister had their own wing of suites that all converged in the chamber that held the Well of Souls. And her sisters spent as little time on Mount Olympus as possible. They would much rather be on the Earth realm partaking in whatever emperor or king's folly rather than here doing their tasks. Atropos would seek the darker pleasures while Clotho sought laughter and parties. Lacy just hoped it stayed that way for a while longer as she attempted and failed to solve the mystery that was the beautiful god that lay in a guest chamber.

"Nani?" She had been so deep in thought she had not even heard him awaken and join her.

Glancing his way, she was once again a bit breathless at his natural predatory allure and beauty. She couldn't help but be transfixed by his muscles as he stretched as if each one was twisting with the next in perfect form. She gave him a smile as she watched him wrap the formasta, the soft white robe of the gods, around that body. The enchanted material transformed to fit him perfectly and would never show a wrinkle or even a tear. Lacy wasn't sure if its molding to his physique was helping or hindering the way he looked. The man was sex incarnate, dressed or undressed, and he didn't even know it, for Mali had not a malicious bone in his body. Again, totally unlike any god she had ever known and Lachesis was realizing her feelings of simply wanting to help the man were becoming something more—wanting the man in ways that had nothing to do with assisting.

She gave him a smile as she rose from the Well of Souls to stand in front of him. "Did you sleep well?"

Mali hated seeing her so exhausted as his lips pressed tightly together in a frown. He reached out to cup her face, saying softly, "I did. But I can see you haven't slept at all."

Before she could protest he was scooping her up into his arms to walk right back into the hallway he had just walked out of. Passing the door to the guest room he was occupying, he reached her door and pushed it open to reveal the beautiful chamber inside. Soft sunlight shone through windows covered in soft, white silk seeming to make the marble walls and floor glow from its touch. Continuing on to the huge bed that seemed to float in mid-air, he laid her down and sat beside her. "Sleep, Nani. I'll be right here to keep watch over you. Or," an almost wicked smile touching his lips, "pin you down if need be. But you will sleep."

Lachesis gave a smile in return as she curled up with her head in his lap before yawning. As Mali's fingers came up to brush softly through her hair, she had to admit a nap sounded divine. But as she lay there, she became aware of the well-muscled thigh under her cheek, the rise and fall of a hardened chest behind her head and the exotic scent of his skin as she breathed it in. Without a thought, she was rolling to her back to press her cheek against the hand to be stroked as her hair had been. Mali gave her the wish, his fingers playing along her brow and then coming down to run feather-light along her jaw. It was if the movements cast a spell as her own hand went up to trace his strong jaw, a soft stubble teasing her fingertips. Her eyes went up to look into his and once again she was mesmerized at their kaleidoscope of color as they phased from a dark grey to an almost purple which caused her to feel heat rush through her blood. She whispered, "Mali..."

It was like just saying his name moved him into action, for he brought her up until their lips met, his hand cradling the back of her neck to angle her mouth to his. The kiss was gentle, almost chaste until his tongue darted out to tease her bottom lip. She sighed as she gave into the invitation as their tongues tasted the other to dance and cause the kiss to increase.

Lachesis had never asked if Mali had tasted and been with all the island and its beautiful tribe offered because she told herself she didn't think of him in such a manner that would merit the question. But as he kissed her, her breath stolen with the arousing sweep of his tongue in the kiss, she was without a doubt wondering now. He had such skill and it didn't take long for her mind to worry about the acquisition of those skills later.

They were now lying back on the bed, Mali's long, lean form half covering her slim, softer one as they couldn't seem to stop kissing. Lachesis ran her hands along his muscled arms to grasp the top of the robe until it slid down to expose his chest. Breaking the kiss, she moved her mouth to lick and tease that perfectly chiseled chest, feeling wanton and bold as she flicked her tongue against his nipples. She had no idea where her body was taking her, as she had never lain with a man, but she just knew she wanted to taste him and make him as breathless as she was.

Mali was completely tempted beyond reason to give into the feelings Lachesis was stirring in him and his body showed it. As she explored with hands and mouth on his chest, it took all the strength he had to pull himself up and off her body, twist and stand next to the bed. He put his head back, blowing out a heated breath to calm himself as he raked his fingers through his hair. "Nani, we shouldn't."

Lachesis was confused as he broke her attentions and now stood out of her reach. Her brow furrowed in confusion and then she whispered softly, "Oh. I must be nothing compared to the beautiful women of the island. I'm sure they were much sweeter fruit than I. How foolish of me." She got to her feet and had only the thought of getting as far away from him as quickly as possible rather than have him see her embarrassment.

Mali reached out to take her wrist to stop her, pulling her back. "No Nani. Not once did I," he couldn't help the amused smile that touched his lips, "taste the fruit the island had to offer. I never laid with anyone. Not that I can remember." He searched her eyes for understanding as his phased from that aroused deep purple to a dark, somber grey. "But you deserve more. You deserve all. And I cannot give that to you. Not sure if I ever could. I won't do that to you."

Something about him thinking of her first and caring that her emotions be the most precious part of this scenario opened up something in Lachesis that she had never felt before. Cherished. Wanted and most of all? She wanted right back. She placed a hand on his chest and said low, in a voice edged with desire, "I'll decide what I deserve."

She pushed with enough force for him to fall back on the bed as she crawled up his body to once again play and tease that chest she had admired for so long. Her other hand dipped under the robe that was gathered at his waist to find his hardened flesh. Mali arched with a moan, all thoughts of protest gone from his mind at her touch. Lachesis had never once touched a man there and she was curious as she rose to her knees, straddling his thighs to make his robe vanish with a thought to see what the fuss was about.

She had seen Mali nude on their first day of meeting, but she had been embarrassed and looked away at his unabashed state. Now she wanted to see and there was a lot to see. His muscles were chiseled as if out of stone on his chest and torso, perfect beneath his olive, tanned skin. A small dark trail of hair began above his belly button and carried down to grow lush and dark as if to draw a path to erotic play. His legs were strong, muscled and long as were his arms that bulged with strength as his hands flexed and unflexed into fists. She had not even seen Greek gods as beautiful as this mysterious man below her.

Her hand was wrapped around a member that was so long and thick her small hand could not even encircle it. It pulsed and throbbed in her hand, and she was fascinated as it seemed to get harder by the second. Or was it her stroking hand that was causing that? She brought her other hand to run through the crisp hairs that nestled at the base and trailed her fingers below to the tight orbs below the shaft. She looked up to meet his eyes, once again dark purple and knew he liked being touched there. It showed in his face, in the way his teeth were biting his bottom lip and the moan that he issued when she gripped tighter and stroked. It was like power and she loved how it was in her hands—literally.

"Do you like what you touch, Nani? See?" His voice was even more exotic and caressing when he was aroused and the sound of it alone was like a caress. She nodded and looked down at her prize once more as her hand moved. Mali let out a low groan as his hips jacked up at her touch before his hand came down to grasp over hers to show how to move it just right. Lachesis was a good student and the flesh got even harder, pulsing as if his heart was held in her hand and if she didn't stop, this was going to be a very fast lesson.

"Can I taste it?"

Mali's head jerked up to look at her and before he could give her an answer, her sweet lips were kissing the tip and then trailing down the shaft in the most delightfully mind numbing way. His hands twisted in her hair as she played, his teeth now locked as he hissed out moans of pleasure. When Lachesis took him in his mouth, he couldn't help the cry of pleasure at the warmth and feeling of her around him. His hands fisted her hair to help her move in ways that felt the best, his hips moving with each lift of and fall of her head as she learned what he taught her.

"Nani..." his voice was a hoarse whisper as tried to form words in a throat that was choked with need, "you must stop or I won't be able to give you the same pleasure." Her head lifted and he thought he heard her give a small whimper at losing what she had so recently been rewarded. He sat up and cupped her face before kissing her deeply, the taste of him on her tongue sending him soaring even higher with need in the fact she and he would become one in more ways very soon.

He laid her back and pulled her hands above her head, able to hold both her slender wrists in one of his hands as he unclasped her robe with his other hand. Tugging, it came away and he looked down at her beauty. And by the gods, was she beautiful.

Her breasts were small but perfect with dusky pink tips that begged to be kissed, which he did. At her soft mew of pleasure, he smiled as he kissed between the rounded flesh to press a kiss on her quivering flat belly. His eyes trailed lower to the apex between her long thighs, which she held tightly together as if embarrassed. He said softly, "Open your legs for me, Nani. Let me see what treasure you seek to hide."

Lachesis couldn't have denied him a thing as she seem to melt beneath his gaze, her thighs softly opening as he moved down, releasing her hands, as his trailed down her body, teasing where his lips had just done the same. "What are you?" but then it was very clear as his mouth kissed one inner thigh and then the other before settling between her thighs. She let out a cry as his lips captured her folds, feeling instantly liquid and warm from the inside out at the touch. She had never felt such an incredibly intoxicating emotion in her whole life. Both her hands thread into his hair only to fist it as the pleasure grew, her hips starting to move under the oral torture he was giving her. She cried out his name as the sensations grew, her fingernails digging into his scalp—she wasn't sure to get him to stop or to do more.

"Not yet, Nani," he growled softly against her flesh as his tongue lapped and drank her sweetness. "I want what you have given no other." And, judging by her surprise, what she hadn't even given to herself. And he wanted her to experience it—to feel the bliss of climax and pleasure.

Lachesis had no idea if she begged or cried as he feasted on her, but soon the feelings were too much and she screamed out his name as something primal seemed to fire in her blood and overtake her. It was like the loosening of the tightest knot inside her body, and its release seem to completely undo her on every level. She thrashed beneath his hands and mouth, losing all sense of what, where and how. But not who, for his name was cried out as each wave drown her in pleasure.

Mali let her orgasm subside before he lifted himself over her body to kiss her with her sweetness still coating his tongue. She moaned in pleasure as his body rubbed over breasts overly-sensitive, skin attuned to his as they touched. He lifted his head as he held himself up on his forearms, brushing her hair away from her brow to meet her eyes. "Nani, do you wish more? I don't wish to take what you are not willing to give. I just wanted to give you pleasure." He somehow knew it was something she denied herself. Pleasure in life, happiness in simple things, and joy in what many took for granted. His Nani was selfless to the core. He bent his head to kiss her neck, whispering against her ear, "I can stop. But only this one time. If we do more, I may not be able to, so tell me sweet Lachesis, do you want me to show you what other pleasure our bodies hold?"

The fates were considered virginal goddesses. It had never been explained to her but she knew it was some caveat that Zeus has ordained—most likely because he liked to keep all the goddesses to himself, related or not. There was so much inbreeding among the gods that aunts married nephews and sister lay with brothers, all in the guise of keeping their superior blood true with breeding. It was sick and not something Lachesis was proud of even knowing. But as this beautiful man above her was offering what she had never dared to take as her own, she knew what the answer would be without a single thought.

"Show me. Please."

CHAPTER SEVEN

Pleasure

The soft spoken words cooled Mali's fire but not the wanting. He knew that Lachesis was a virgin and for all he knew, so was he. But he knew that was highly unlikely, because even though his mind had no memory, his body seemed to recall all too well how to pleasure a woman. He forced his mind away from that—for it was that very thing that had prevented him bedding a female before. What if he had a wife? Children? No, that was not to enter in this chamber, he forbid it from invading this moment. Lachesis was helping him without asking anything in return and this, this he could give her.

And he wanted to, more than anything in the world.

So as she spoke the words, he found himself once more searching those beautiful eyes for any sign of fear and found none. Kissing her deeply, his hand slid between them, nails raising goose bumps on her flesh in his path. Reaching between her legs, he let his fingers tease the flesh he had feasted on, finding it welcoming and wet as he readied her. Her breath went into gasps and moans as he once again led her to the edge of climax. His fingers worked her flesh to get it ready for his own as he kissed her, drinking in her moans as if they were ambrosia and he would be exalted to a higher level of being with the sound.

He broke the kiss to say softly, "This will hurt but for a moment. But then Nani, the doors of pleasure will open and sweep us both away to a shore we both seek." He cupped her face as he kissed her again, moving his hand to grip her hip as he slid his hardness against her, rubbing across her folds and nub of pleasure. She arched up with a cry as her hands grabbed his shoulders, nails digging into his skin until blood surfaced beneath them. He hissed out in pleasure at that as he lifted his hips to claim her body as his.

At first he thought he was too large for her, she was so delicate and small, as he inserted himself so slowly, letting her stretch to take him in until he felt the resistance of her virginity barring his invasion. He felt her tense and he kissed her again as he pressed deeper into her body, and then the barrier gave way and he was sliding inside.

Lachesis had never felt something so powerful, until the pain. She tightened her grip on his shoulders and let out a small cry of fear until he kissed her, causing the panic to disappear. Then she felt him inside of her as the pain gave way to something more. He felt huge but it was a fullness that made her feel more complete and alive. As if that void of womanhood was now filled as it was created to be by a man worthy to do so. A man that at this very moment made her a woman in every way.

Mali.

An unknown god with a forgotten past. A being of such heart and yet so strong that she was sure no other god could stand against him if he had knowledge to tap into the power hidden inside. A man with such a caring nature that as she realized the gift he was giving, she felt tears course down her cheeks as he began to move. Lachesis was falling in love...

Mali had his head on her shoulder as his hips moved slowly, restraining the need to thrust and conquer out of care for her being new to making love. It was then, when he felt the soft, warm wetness of her tears against his neck causing him to look over at her. "Nani?" He kissed her tears as he cupped her face, stilling his hips afraid she still felt the pain. Or was regretting giving him such a precious gift as her maidenhead. "Do you wish me to stop?"

Lachesis shook her head for the last thing she wanted was for him to stop. "No. I have just never felt this way." She hoped he would take that to mean the experience of pleasure rather than the reality of her heart in the mix. "Please, more. Don't stop."

He smiled gently and captured her mouth, tongue sweeping to meet hers as if to assure her that he understood even though she knew he had no way of knowing the truth of it all. But then he started moving again, but this time more urgent and her brain once again shut off to let her body reign over this experience.

Mali's thrusts became harder and more demanding as his hips ground into hers, plunging into flesh that gripped him as tightly as the moment held them both. Soon he was groaning with each sink into her flesh and she was moaning with every rise. Her legs came up to wrap around his waist as her hands once again dug into his shoulders, scraping and marking his perfect skin with trails of nails leading into blood. She gripped the scars on his back and it only seemed to fuel him more as he became almost animalistic as she became more intense. Gone was the sweetness of the first time as it was ripped away by a storm of the darkest need for submission and give.

Mali rolled to his back as Lachesis mounted him, their hips never stopping the demands of their bodies as he did. She was so beautiful in wild abandonment with her head falling back, long dark hair whisper soft against his thighs as she braced her hands on his chest, nails digging in there as well. Her lips were swollen from their kisses, her skin a hue of pink from the arousal and he was completely under her unknown spell. His hips rose to thrust harder as she demanded more with wicked twists of her hips. For someone who knew not of lovemaking, she was apparently gifted by the very gods she was a part of in the act of it. Soon, he could no longer drink in the sight of his lover as passion overtook him, causing his eyes to close, his mouth to open and moans from them both filling the air. His hands gripped her hips tight as he felt his own climax building, making him swell and seek for hers.

Lachesis felt the change in him and knew that she would be joining him in what would be a soul shattering end to their deed, for she felt that loosening even more so with him buried deep inside of her. Dropping down to cover his body with her own, she kissed him as he seem to tighten up, muscle rolling on his bones to stop her from moving.

Then it happened and he threw back his head to roar out her name, his body bowing up as he pulled her harder against him where their bodies joined. Lachesis would have liked to enjoy the sight of his orgasm on that beautifully handsome face, but her own climax hit her and she was clinging to him with arms and legs as he thrashed as she got lost in her own.

And her heart followed right along and she knew she was lost in more ways than one.

CHAPTER EIGHT

Fall

Lachesis must have watched Mali sleep for what felt like hours. Both were totally sated after making love three times and then falling asleep in each other's arms. She had awoken to him wrapped tightly around her, his face so soft in sleep that she couldn't bear to wake him up. Not that she minded the view at all—the man was absolutely glorious to look upon. And now, he was hers. That thought made her smile softly as she leaned in to kiss his lips, causing him to stir in his sleep.

She used that moment to unwind from his arms, stretching as she stood next to the bed. He was sprawled on her bed, his size just as intimating on the large bed as it was in any other way, even in sleep. Completely male and totally sensual with sheets twisted around his legs and even now, his manhood growing hard under her gaze. The man was insatiable and she did not mind that a bit. She could completely see why her sisters and the other gods gave into the more carnal desires of the flesh. And as soon as he woke, she planned on partaking on them once more.

Picking up her robe off the floor, she pulled it on as she hummed happily, wrapping her arms around herself as she made her way to the courtyard where the morning sun shone bright amidst the colorful lit flowers. It was as she was passing the chamber of Souls that Lachesis felt it.

A soul calling to her, like a siren's song to the heart that only she and her sisters could hear. She attempted to ignore it, but that would mean one of her sisters would be drawn from Earth to answer the call, so she entered the chamber and walked over to the Well of Souls. Sitting on its edge, she ran her hand under the surface of the water, closing her eyes and calling back to the soul that beckoned her. Her brow creased in puzzlement as the sensation from the approaching thread was different—like nothing she had felt before. It was as if the thread itself was far stronger than even she, and it was pulling her under the water rather than her it. Her eyes snapped open in alarm as if she truly was being pulled under, the sensation being so great. A thick, pulsing, glowing thread surfaced but it seemed to be more alive than just a thread. It snaked out and coiled around her hand and she was hit with so much power it sent her stumbling to her feet and then her knees, crying out in alarm.

As soon as it wrapped around her wrist and fingers, flashes of memories, a past, a present and a future exploded in her mind at such an alarming rate she grew dizzy and swayed. This thread was never meant to be found and it had been hidden by powers far greater than she. Crying out as the imagery seemed to rupture her mind; she welcomed the dark escape as she passed out and collapsed on the floor.

Mali was having the most delightful dream about he and Lachesis back on the island where she had found him. They were laughing in the surf after making love on the beach. His dream self was about to do so again when suddenly he was awoke seconds before he went flying through the air to hit one of the marble walls of Lachesis' bed chamber. Hitting the floor in a heap, he jumped to his feet in a fighting stance seconds before he was hit with what he could only think was a ball of energy that slammed him right back into that same wall, this time slumping to the floor in a daze.

"See Father, I told you Lachesis had a guest. A male guest, too."

Mali lifted his head, shaking it to clear to see three men and two women standing at the opening of Lachesis' chambers. One of the men was huge, dark-haired wearing a scowl on a cruel mouth, another almost too pretty to look at with shining blonde hair, and the final male older, with elegant white beard and lightning bright eyes. The two women with them were beautiful—one blonde with sparkling blue eyes while the other a redhead and curvy with flashing green eyes. And all dressed, unlike him.

He struggled to get to his feet, only for the huge man to appear before him and force him to his knees. He rolled his eyes up at the man and hissed out, "I get on my knees for no man."

The man laughed and clamped a hand tight on his shoulder, the grip like iron as he said in a booming voice, "You will and shall bow for the king of the gods, Zeus. Who is not a man, but an almighty god."

Mali's eyes went wide as he looked at the older man. So this was the god that Lachesis had feared would learn of his presence here. The man seemed to crackle with energy as if the air itself was wielded to his will and leaving nothing but vapor for everyone else. Mali grabbed the arm of the man who pinned him and with a show of force, stood in spite of the man's strength to spin and press him face first against the wall. "Let me rephrase that then. I go to my knees for no one, god or otherwise."

"Stop!" Zeus voice seemed to shake the walls of the temple and Mali stepped away, grabbing a cloth from a side table to wrap around his hips. The big man shoved away from the wall and tapped shoulders angrily as he walked past to once again stand at the god king's side. Mali faced them and rolled his head, discreetly looking around for Lachesis, hoping she stayed away as this little meet and greet continued.

"Who are you?"

He narrowed his eyes at Zeus' question and shrugged, answering simply, "I don't know. They call me Mali. That is the only name I know."

The two women whispered an odd look of confusion on their faces. Zeus glanced at them and pointed before barking at them, "Tell me fates, who is this dog standing in your sister's temple?"

The fates whispered between themselves and moved past Zeus to come and stand in front of him. He looked from one to the other as they circled him, whispering a strange language he did not understand. Occasionally, they would reach out and touch him, ever so lightly but it made him want to move away from it. It was not like Lachesis' gentle touch, for her sister's touch felt more invasion and sinister.

"Stop that," he hissed as they continued their almost clinical inspection. His eyes darted past them to the other door to Lachesis' chamber, now wishing she would come in and stop this strange examination by her sisters.

The two fates stopped and then backed away from him, pointing before speaking to Zeus as if in a trance and in unison. "He has no past. No present and no future. He is a god with no name. A god without a people or a temple of worship. But a god of great power though that power is untapped." Their tones went to an awed hushed whisper, "More power than even you, mighty Zeus."

Zeus bellowed out in rage and everyone seemed to cower and scurry away from his wrath. Except for Mali, for he had no idea what any of them were talking about. But Zeus seemed to be worked up into a lather as he walked up and backhanded him so hard he spun and crashed into a trunk of some kind—it, its contents and him tumbling to the floor. Zeus was on him in seconds, pointing a very wicked bolt-shape cut sword at his throat. "Did you dare sully a fate? Did you lay with her and take her with your worthless body? Tell me!"

Mali glared up at the god, his lips curling off his teeth, showing his fangs. He smiled and hissed out, "I did. And she didn't find it worthless. Nor did I find hers less than perfect."

Zeus let out another bellow as he reached down and grabbed him by the throat as if he weighed nothing, shaking him like a doll before throwing him the opposite way across the chamber. Another trunk paid the price as he came crashing down on it. As Mali struggled to his feet, the large man was now taking his turn as a meaty fist planted in his stomach, sending all the air out of his lungs. He shoved the man away only to be faced by blondie who kicked him in the chest and sent him sliding across the floor.

Mali was trying to keep in mind that this was his Nani's family—but with each body part that ached that thought was scattering fast. Flipping up, he charged with a snarl the shiny one and they slammed against a wall, with Mali's arms wrapped around him. He brought a fist back and punched, feeling a satisfying crunch of nose under his knuckles. The big man grabbed him and pulled him off the blonde one as he wrapped an arm around his throat in a choke hold to pick him off his feet, suspended in the air by the hold.

Mali struggled but the big man was strong and it only took less than a minute to see black streaks in his vision as his air failed him. Blondie walked over and started throwing one punch after the other into his gut and soon he was nothing more than a dazed punching bag for their entertainment. When he was let go, he folded up and crumbled to the floor, laying there gasping to breathe. Zeus walked over and planted a boot on his chest and leaned on the knee to glare down at him.

"The punishment for being in my holy place without permission is death. The punishment for soiling a virgin goddess is death. The punishment for angering me is death." A slow smile spread across Zeus' lips as he spoke, looking forward to carrying out those punishments as he raised that odd sword, lightening sparking along the edges.

Lachesis came to with a gasp, that strange blue thread still pulsing on her wrist. Sitting up, she unwrapped it and held it close. She knew everything about Mali now. His past, what he was.

Who he was.

And now she feared for him far more than she did before. Before he was an unknown entity with no consequence or path. Now that she knew what she did, he would never be safe again. Or kind. She got to her feet and let the thread float near the edge of the Well.

That was when she heard it. A crash and the grating bellow of Zeus. In her chamber.

Where Mali was.

"No!" She screamed just seconds before Zeus' lightning blade struck Mali, who was pinned under the god's boot. She ran over and grabbed Zeus to pull him away, glancing down at a beaten and half-conscious Mali. She turned her glare to her cousins, Apollo and then Hephaestus. "How dare you come into my private chambers and assault my guest!" She turned her anger to her two sisters, narrowing her eyes and knew one of them must have found out and told.

"Why?" She put herself between Zeus and Mali as her two sisters straightened their spines, their faces turning to that of snide and confidence.

Atropos answered first. "We heard the thread calling. But when we came, we sensed the unknown. We saw him and you know the rules. So we let Zeus know you had a guest. A guest he was not aware of. We simply followed the rules."

Clotho nodded and answered in a sarcastic sing-song voice, "The rules are very important, aren't they, Zeus?" Before Zeus could respond, Lachesis let out a snort of bitter laughter. "You two are now finding the rules important? After playing and bedding any handsome human you could find, now you are spouting the rules?" "Lachesis!" Zeus turned his anger on her but she refused to cower. Zeus knew, just as the other gods, that their threads were no more resistant to the manipulations of the Fates than any human, creature or otherwise. "You will not fault your sisters for needing time away from their duties. We all partake of the pleasure of earth. But this," he stepped up closer to her, his eyes sparking with energy held barely in check, "is not earth. This is Mount Olympus and here my rules are iron and rock. Not to be bent and never broken."

Lachesis opened her mouth to retort that all of them did it. Constantly ran sex partners in and out of their chambers as most people did dogs for walks. But as Mali let out a weak groan behind her, she knew she had to switch tactics or Zeus would carry out his punishment. Praying it worked, she stepped up to Zeus and laid her hand on his chest, looking up at him coyly.

"You are right. But this toy wasn't important enough to waste the time as such a mighty god as you. He is so lowly that he didn't merit breathing the same air as you or seeing your magnificent chambers to be greeted." She gave a smile and trailed her fingers up to toy with his beard. "I'm finished with him anyway. It was just a brief dalliance to relieve my boredom and stress. Perhaps you could assist me and send him back to earth? I would be so very grateful my King." She met his eyes as she pressed herself against him, bile rising up in her throat as she did so. She knew Zeus was as vane and self-serving as all the other gods combined, so she played on those weaknesses, hoping he would take the bait and Mali would be sent back alive.

Zeus smiled and grasped her chin to stroke her jaw with his thumb, "You think me a fool little fate? I will grant your wish. But not in the way you request." He moved past her and Lachesis turned to watch him in confusion. Zeus stood over Mali as the man tried to get to his feet, his ever changing eyes meeting hers. Lachesis breath caught when she realized he had heard all that she said. Her eyes pled with him but already his eyes were turning a thunderous red. He bared his teeth as he got to his feet, "Nani? That's not true. Tell me that is not true!"

Zeus looked between the two of them, greatly amused as he waited for her to answer. Lachesis had to be careful. Mali was a simple bolt away from being turned to ash from one of Zeus' lightning bolts. She sighed and stood up straight, bringing up a nail to look at. "You were nothing. I wanted a lover of skill for my first time and I had no doubt you would fit that need. Now that need is done. I'm finished with you."

It broke her heart to see Mali's face crumble, his eyes fade from the fighting red to a funeral like grey. He shook his head and whispered, "It's not true. You're lying. I can hear it in your voice." He turned his gaze to Zeus. "She's saying what you want to hear. If you want to punish, then do so, but no way will I believe her words. Do what you must."

Zeus smiled and grabbed Mali by the throat as an opening appeared at his feet. Lachesis screamed in protest, but Apollo and Hephaestus held her back by the arms. "No! Zeus! I beg you! Please!"

It was then that Mali knew he had been right. The love that showed in Lachesis face was clear and he started to struggle, to what means he had no idea.

But when her cousins grabbed her, he roared out for them to let her go. Zeus snorted and then let him go to tumble through the clouds and down to the earth below.

"Good bye dog. Enjoy the fall."

CHAPTER NINE

Brother

"**Y**ou have lost your little demon fucking mind. No being falls from the sky, crashes through earth and lands in hell." The demon cowered with a squeak and pointed as the dark lord was seconds away from blasting the disgusting, ugly creature into goop.

Lucifer followed the pointed shaking claw to a being lying broken on the stone floor of the realm. The man was laying on his side, with his back to them and that's when he saw two long healed jagged scars on the man's shoulders and knew the demon wasn't insane. For only one being could survive such a fall.

He should know.

He bellowed, throwing two lesser demons off of the man as they began chewing on flesh. He pointed at them all as he snarled, "Get away from him! Do not touch him!" They all scurried away, shaking against the walls at his commands. He knelt next to the man who laid on the floor, bloodied and shattered, to gently turn him over. The bones were broken, the skin split and even though he had not seen his face in eons, before the dawn of modern religion, he knew it as he knew his own.

His touch was gentle as he brushed hair from the man's forehead, his heart breaking for the abuse that had been heaped upon him, along with the damage from the fall. He whispered softly, "I thought you had been destroyed." Lucifer grabbed a demon and snarled at it, "Get my chambers ready and the best healers we have. Now!"

Mali's eyes opened just a slit as he heard the rough and commanding voice above him. He hurt all over and he felt like every bone in his body was cracked. He tried to focus on the speaker but his gaze was all a fuzzed blur that he was not sure was even reality based.

Lucifer looked down to see he was awake and gave him a gentle smile as he said softly, "Brother, you live. Stay still, I can help you." The dark lord then brought his own wrist up to bite with his fangs, blood coursing down his arm as he held it out to Mali. "Drink."

Mali gave the strange being a look of disgust, eyes rolling away as he felt like he was going to black out again. He grimaced and croaked out, "No."

Lucifer grabbed him by the hair to yank his head up crudely to his bleeding wrist. "You have to drink or you will die. Our blood is the same and I have more than I need and you have very little. Now drink you fucking fool."

Mali sickened at the thought but had no idea why he latched on to the being's wrist and did as he was told. The blood was hot like fire with a strong sizzling feel on his tongue but as soon as it hit his throat the pain vanished and his mind slowed to a slurred pace. Dropping back as the being pulled his arm away, he whispered through the haze that was making him numb, "Who are you?"

Lucifer frowned deeply, pained that the man did not know him. How was that possible after all they had been through together? Gently placing his knuckles to feel Mali's pulse, he said softly, "Do you not know me brother?"

Mali weakly shook his head as he felt darkness stealing him away. "No, I don't know who you are. Why do you call me Brother?"

Lucifer watched him pass out and stood as the healers came running with the stretcher. "Because that, my friend, is what you are."

"What did you do to him?"

It wasn't often that the Omega had a visit from Lucifer, so to have the dark lord appear before him was surprising to say the least. "Who Lucifer, did I do what to?"

Lucifer snorted and paced as the Omega, the father to all, sat on his padded chair, reading a book. "Our mutual friend. He lives and came crashing into hell from on high. I thought he was dead, destroyed."

It didn't take Omega long to realize whom the devil was talking about as he sat his book down, splaying his hand on it. A tome that had not even been published, and would not be for over another 2000 years. Looking up at the dark lord, the father of all, lord of light smiled. "I don't believe I once said your brother was destroyed or killed. You assumed he was."

The Omega rose to place a hand on Lucifer's shoulder, to say softly, "We both know why that is not so. He was mere scapegoat to your greed and lust. But could not go unpunished. I am not without mercy."

Lucifer wrenched his shoulder away from Omega's touch to sneer at him, spitting out each word, "You could have told me. All these centuries I thought he was gone. I," yelled out the words, "thought he was dead! I mourned what I had caused. Raged against the loss. And he was on earth the whole time!"

Omega gave the devil a look of both understanding and grief, for the dark lord was not the only one who felt sadness about how their worlds were ripped apart and had to be rebuilt. "That was your punishment."

Lucifer snarled, his lips curling off dangerously long fangs as he regarded the so-called good half of the equation of all. Omega was the one being stronger than even he, but the temptation to slaughter the being was so overwhelming at that moment, Lucifer had to dig his nails into his palms as he curled his fingers into fists to prevent doing so. Perhaps some grain of his emotions should be grateful his brother had not been destroyed, but in a way, that wasn't totally true. "He doesn't know me. Doesn't know what he is. Who he was. Why?"

Omega turned to run his fingers along his chair, deep in thought before answering. Glancing at Lucifer, he said softly, "Atonement. Many of your own kind and my own family were lost in your scheme. Mankind was brought to the brink of destruction. And unknowingly or not, you both had to pay. It's my nature and that which I cannot go against any more than you or any other purpose being. So, I removed his past and gave him a new beginning without it. Hoping his true nature would find redemption and for the right of man once more. But I could not allow his need for revenge against you to stand in the way. And such power as your brother has?" He shook his head and looked down at the book that now rested under his fingers. "Could not go unchecked. So it had been locked from even he."

Part of Lucifer completely got why Omega had done, but he still mourned for a brother found but still lost to even himself. Sitting down, he dropped his head down to cover his face with his hands, saying low as he did so, "How can he be unlocked? What can I do? It's my fault he was involved to begin with. My fault he was set up, which you already know." He dropped his hands; suddenly weary, to look at Omega. "How does he get his true self returned to him? To me? I want my brother back, as he should be."

Omega took his seat and regarded Lucifer. "As he should be? Or how he was when you two were last together?"

Lucifer had to think on that one and it was not an easy task to do. His brother and he were a powerful force that had laid waste to all they sought to destroy. But he also remembered how his brother lost his good, his nature to be kind and save rather than harm. Blowing out a slow breath, he shrugged. "As he was born to be. My opposite. Light."

Omega gave a proud smile and reached out to touch Lucifer's arm. "Then he must redeem himself to mankind. He must find that nature without his powers and then his true self will be reborn and remembered."

Lucifer's brown creased in thought and then nodded. "I have just the way. But you must assure me that if that way does indeed save mankind, for good and the light, you will fully restore his powers. Give back to him what has been locked away."

Omega tilted his head and gave a nod. "On the light, I promise. But he cannot be told. Nor can you show him in anyway his past or identity. The result must be a natural turning of events. Not manipulated."

Lucifer stood and held out his hand and the Omega took it in his own. "Agreed. For the light."

CHAPTER TEN

Touch of Fate

It had taken her far too long to make her way back to the Well of Souls. First a lecture from Zeus and then her sisters trying to validate why they were bitches. All Lachesis could think was to hide Mali's thread before anyone else could find it and see who the man was. And the power he held. As she was running back to the Well's chamber, she was confronted by Atropos in the hallway, obstructing the entrance to it.

"Care to explain, little sister?" Atty held her shears in her fingers, twirling them as if a toy and not an instrument to end a life with a simple snip. Lachesis' eyes went to them and felt fear that Atropos may have done something to the very thread Lachesis was trying so desperately to hide. If Mali has even survived the fall, which was an even greater fear. No one survived the fall from Zeus' hand.

Lachesis narrowed her eyes, while casting her senses to the Well and felt internal relief that Clotho was not inside and the strange energy from Mali's thread still pulsed within. Could not her sisters feel it? Or was it because she and Mali had touched souls when they were one in her bed? She had no idea, but she knew she must carry out protecting him and that thread was the key to do so.

Lachesis stepped up close to her sister, wrapping her fingers around the shears to stop their annoying turn. She met her sister's eyes and spat out, "I do not have to explain myself to you or anyone. You are the last one to demand it from me. Let me guess Atty, did you even bother washing off the last orgy you were at before you came here to tattle to Zeus? Or is there another lover or two waiting for you in your chambers?" She let the shears go and stepped back. "Now move or we shall see which of us can be the bigger bitch."

Atty laughed in amusement but did not move. "By the gods, you getting laid and losing your precious virginity has done you well. Look how much spine you have after laying under a man." It was only then that Atty moved out of Lachesis way. Glancing at her sister, she said softly, her voice almost sounding kind, "What Zeus did was too much. But you should have known any unknown god would be destroyed. Zeus does not like the unknowns. Even if that unknown was beautiful to the eye. I'm sorry for my part in his demise, sister."

Lachesis regarded Atty in puzzlement. The coldest and harshest of the three, she was shocked to see even the hint of regret from her sister fate. It baffled her to a level where she had no idea how to respond, so she gave a simple nod and then entered the chamber, closing the door behind her.

Mali had no idea how long he had been unconscious, only that when he came out of it, a healer would torment him more by stitching and stripping damaged flesh, or checking for healing and finding very little. For all Mali knew, days, weeks, years may have passed by as he lay in this strange place in agony.

"Why is he not healing?"

Mali's eyes cracked open once more at the sound of the man who called himself his brother, trying to focus on what he and the healer were discussing.

The healer looked at him and then back at its master. "I do not know, Sire. We have tried all we know to do. And you have given more blood than I would recommend. The injuries are grave, yet he does not die. Nor does he heal. We shall continue to try what we must."

Mali watched as the dark one grabbed the demon to haul him off his feet, snarling in his face, "If he dies? So do you. And anyone else that failed to save him." The demon was dropped in a heap and scurried to press itself against a well, shaking in fear as a nod was given in understanding as its Master left them alone.

Mali frowned in confusion as to why the dark being cared or even knew him, but that thought was apparently too much for his pain-blurred mind and he gave into the darkness once more as the demon came forward with some tool of "healing".

Lachesis stared at Mali's thread as it swirled in the water. "Show him to me."

The water went murky and then seem to steam as it manifested Mali's location. She gasped when she saw how injured he was. He was lying on his stomach and the scars on his back had burst open, bleeding and raw. His whole body seemed to have been battered and bloodied. She had her fingers over her mouth to keep from crying, but was also thrilled to see he did indeed still live. Somehow, some way, he had survived the fall. And a new fear bloomed—if Zeus and the other found out he did, they would put a death bounty on Mali's head. One that would remain until the man was dead.

Focusing on where he was, her eyes glowed white as she used all of her powers to determine his location. It wasn't on earth for then her powers would barely be tapped. No, it was a realm not of her own Parthenon, which meant forbidden to her and the other Greek deities. She gasped when she realized where he had landed as the images faded. She would go to see him, nonetheless, but it would be dangerous if she was discovered—but she knew she had to. Her heart would drive her mad if she did not.

As the vision faded, she was left watching his thread and knew she had to make sure no one found it and used what she had learned from it. But how?

Mali deserved to know his past and the power he was ordained to carry. The destiny and all it entailed. But how to hide it so neither her sisters nor anyone with the power of fate could sense and read? Biting a nail in frustration, she looked to the Well for some answers but it only swirled waiting for her command. She was the only one that knew Mali's true past and self; but that wasn't true, whoever had taken such efforts to hide it had to be powerful and know it as well. That's when she knew what she had to do. Holding her hand over the water, the thread swirled around the walls of the Well as she said softly with tears gently falling to mix with the water in which it spun, "Show me his future."

"Mali. Wake up. Please?"

He thought he imagined the gentle voice along with the calming touch, blaming it on his misery, until he felt the softest lips touch his. His eyes fluttered open, threatening to close once more as he met her eyes, a smile trying to form on his lips, as his voice croaked out, "Nani?"

Lachesis was kneeling beside his bed, her fingers gently brushing though his long, dark hair. "It's me." He tried to rise and she quickly pressed him to stay, alarmed it was easily done with him being so weak. "Don't get up. You're hurt very badly. You need to heal."

He swallowed back the nausea and shook his head. "They say I do not heal. Nor do I die."

Lachesis was not surprised—Zeus had every intention to destroy Mali, death from the fall. But with Mali being what he was, the wish of a Greek god, even one as mighty as Zeus, would not have had its full effect. So now Mali held the pain, the injury from the god king's hand, but not the end result. "It's because your injury was done from a god. But not of your own, so only a god of that pantheon can heal you." Lachesis laid her hand along his arm, with the other gently still stroking his hair, "I can begin the healing, but it will take time."

Her hands grew warm and she closed her eyes as she put all her energy remaining into starting the process. She knew it was working when Mali let out a sigh of relief and pleasure as the pain started to whisper away, his tight muscles relaxing beneath her hand, the heat from his brow lessening as the fever gave up its hold.

His body shuddered as the blinding aches and pains faded, his eyes opening to become clearer and focused. "Nani? Are you here to take me back to the island? Or somewhere new with you?"

Lachesis heart broke at his simple, almost pitiful request and she laid her forehead on his. "No, Mali. I can't. They will be hunting you and they can find me far too easy." It was true, for she and her sisters were connected as three of the same power. Even more reason for her doing what she had done to keep his secret as it should be, even from him. "I wish I could. More than I can ever say. But this is goodbye."

Mali blinked, afraid his hearing was not working right; as his brows came down to try to analyze her words. "Goodbye? Why? I don't understand."

Lachesis couldn't help the tears that formed and then fell as she struggled to speak, the pain in her heart from finding love and then now losing it, almost too much to allow it to beat. "I have to do whatever it takes to protect you. To keep you safe." She lifted her head to meet those beautiful eyes as they were phasing to dark grey. Would she never have another chance to decipher their hues and changes? No, this would be the last time to look into their kaleidoscope. "But I know you will find love. And happiness. I promise that. It just won't be with me. No matter how much I wish it."

Mali struggled to rise, finding his strength was returning, albeit in a small amount. Sitting, he took her arms in his hands and looked into her eyes as she rose with him. "Nani, no. We'll run away. Go back to the island. Find another island. Whatever you want! I do not want to go back to being alone. To being without you. I know you feel you are doing what is right, but don't do this. Don't leave me here. In this place. Please."

Lachesis cupped his face and kissed him, then held him tightly to her. She was unsure if it was to keep him close or to avoid seeing the pain and pleading in his eyes. "I have to, Mali. I hate it. But I have to." She pulled back and kissed him again. "Forgive me. Please forgive me."

Mali gripped her arms tighter, his voice edged with not only anguish but anger. "Nani. No. Do not do this, Lachesis. You are more than just a fate. You are a woman I want to love. Please, do not do this." He shook her slightly, her tears only making him feel more helpless—he could tell this was not what she wanted, but what she felt she must do. She was wrong, he knew it. "Nani. Do not let them destroy what we could be!"

"I can't, Mali." She was sobbing now, pulling away and stepping back. "I have to do this. I'm so sorry."

Mali glared at her, trying to get to his feet, only to have his legs give. He growled out the words, desperate to stop her at the same time, "You leave me. Like this, I will never forgive you. Do you hear me Goddess of Fate? Never."

Lachesis couldn't even look at him as he grew angrier. She turned and ran out the door and down the hall, wishing she could shut out the sounds of him screaming for her to come back.

"You know, it's not often I am blessed with someone so beautiful and powerful in my realm." He rolled his head as he cracked his neck. "Without my permission and not in my bed."

Lucifer stood in front of the Fate as she almost ran straight into him, most likely because she was crying like a lost child as she did so. He smiled as he leaned a shoulder against the wall, crossing his arms as he looked her from head to foot and back up. "So, you're the reason he had to fall."

Lachesis knew who the powerful being in front of her was. She also knew this was his realm and she was forbidden from being here not being from his circle of deities. In fact, most likely, none were welcome in his realm. His ruthlessness and cruelty had even reached the Greeks whispered rumored mills. She stood up straight, quickly wiping the tears from her eyes before meeting his. "I am. And you're the reason he's alive."

Lucifer smiled, tilted his head and gave a nod. "I am. Feel free to show your gratitude in any way you wish. I accept sex. In fact, I endorse it."

Lachesis recoiled at his crudeness, stepping back from him. "No, thank you. But nice of you to offer. Why did you save him?"

Lucifer narrowed his gaze as fire started to lick in the blue of his eyes. He took strides to force her back against the wall, bracing his hands on either side of her head. "You come into my realm and you honestly think you can ask one fucking thing of me? I can kill you. Right here, right now and no one would know. It is my right to do so for your invasion."

He glanced down the hall at Mali's bellows and then down at her. "Bitch, you caused him more pain. Do you get off on that? Or is it just a sick legacy of your weak vanishing kind?" He came in close to hiss, eyes going down to her lips. "Leave him alone. If you give one bit of care for him beyond spreading your legs, never see him again."

Lachesis sorrow burned away in the rage of how he was talking to her as she planted a hand on his chest to push him back. "You are one to talk. Considering what you did to him. I'm not the first that caused him to fall, now am I?" As soon as the words were spoken, she saw his look. How could she reveal she knew Mali's past? To this being of all beings.

Lucifer's eyes went wide as he grabbed her arm and hauled her up against him, the heat off his body searing even to Lachesis as his rage licked up, shown as flames in his eyes. A beautiful, deadly creature of pure evil. "How did you know that?" He came in low and pressed his lips against her neck, his fangs nipping her pulse. "You just sealed his death. And any hope I had in saving him, bitch."

She once again shoved him away, but his hold on her arm remained, fingers digging into her skin, hot and wicked. "You? Save him? You doomed him before, why do you wish to save him now?"

She was right of course. He let her go and backed away, crossing his arms on his chest before looking down at the floor. "What if I told you I have a plan that will not only save him, but give him back what he has lost?" He looked up at her and his had voice taken on an almost caring tone. Something Lachesis thought him incapable of.

"A plan? He can't leave this place! The moment he does, Zeus and the others will kill him. They will put a death bounty on his head. Will your plan prevent that? Keep him safe?" Lachesis felt odd having hope that the devil would say the truth and give such, but it was all she had. And she was grasping at it in total desperation. "What do you need from me?"

Lucifer smiled but it was far from friendly. More like a snake about to devour its prey. "Easy. I need you to forget all that you know since I assume your sisters can find out, since you three bitches work together. I need you to make sure you will never remember. And finally," he stepped up close once more to look into her eyes, "stay away from him."

CHAPTER ELEVEN

A Purpose

"**Y**ou look well, Mali."
He looked over at Lucifer and looked back down at his hands as he unwrapped the sparring wraps. "Don't call me that."

Lucifer's brow went up and he smirked, stepping into the fight room to sit across from his brother. "Oh that's right. Your new name, if one can call it a name, is Bounce. It's ridiculous."

He looked at Lucifer and returned the smirk, eyes going back down as he tossed the wraps, flexing his knuckles, "You little minions gave it to me. It stuck. And I'm not that stupid ignorant god I once was."

Lucifer let out a chuckle as he sat back, lacing his hands in his lap. "They called you Bounce as a joke. They had never seen anyone bounce when they hit earth from a spiraling free fall and then bounce again as they crashed into hell. They actually thought it might be the most amazing meal delivery system ever invented. They were sadly disappointed when I didn't let them eat their bouncing treat."

But Bounce, as his brother now called himself did indeed look much better. The injuries and damage from the fall had all healed without scars except for two. The two horrific jagged scars on his shoulders had once again closed up and healed, but still remained as before. Bounce had cut his long hair to be but a few inches on his head, most likely to not draw notice, but it had the opposite effect— his strange eyes stood out even more so in his beautifully handsome face, so anyone would immediately be mesmerized by their changing colors. Lucifer assumed that the Fate's visit was what has begun the healing two weeks ago, and for that he was grateful. Not that he would ever tell the goddess that. Or thank anyone for anything for that matter.

"I owe you."

Lucifer looked up at Bounce and tilted his head, "You do. And I have how you will pay me back. And it will give you purpose. One that I feel will occupy your time and your energy to the point of having neither. And it will keep those bastard Greeks from taking your lovely head."

Bounce rolled his shoulders, wondering if the ache they held would ever go away as he regarded Lucifer. The being hadn't called him brother since he had first come here and he had not asked why he had done so then. Bounce knew he was the devil, but he also knew the dark lord had given him haven as well as been most gracious to him during his stay. But Lucifer was right—he was restless and ready to do something. He felt like he had wasted so much time laying around on an island with no cares that he wanted to start doing the opposite now. That and to forget a certain goddess who had left him here.

"I won't hurt humans nor will I harm innocents." His eyes lifted to Lucifer's as he said it firmly. "If that is what you wish, then think of something else. I won't do it."

Lucifer smiled, bringing up his fingers to toy with a blood jewel ring on his finger, "Now, you wound me to think I would ask such a thing. Not to mention those are my hobbies; I don't share well."

Bounce snorted and walked over to pour himself a glass of water, pointing as he poured. "Drink?"

Lucifer smiled as he manifested his own jeweled silver goblet, swirling the liquid inside of it. "No, thank you. I have my own special brew." Bringing the goblet to his lips, he took a deep drink, licking blood from his lips as he lowered it. "So, here is your new purpose to pay back your debt." He waited until Bounce sat and explained. "There is now a treaty between my realm and Heaven. A war wages that is beyond both realms control and mankind is paying the price. There is a new sector of demons that are feeding on the humans, sadly enough, led by my own blood. These demons use the human spark to exist on earth, such lousy design that they are, they can't sustain on that realm without it due to mankind's energy. They can then become by appearance, if they wish the humans they eat. They wish to destroy mankind and claim Earth as their own once it's plunged into darkness without the light of man, since they are not welcome in Hell and Heaven wants them gone. I want you to lead an army to erase them from existence and in exchange," he thought before saying carefully, "I will grant you things you dare not even ask for now."

He leveled his gaze at Bounce. "So don't bother asking now. Just know that you will pay your debt to me when the war has ended as I wish. And by leading this army, you are saving mankind. The Greeks won't touch you while you are doing this purpose, for unlike us, they need mankind's worship to exist. And to make an attempt on your life, since you are serve both Heaven and Hell, will mean they will be killed for doing so."

Bounce once again gave Lucifer a look of disgust at his drink of choice but then went into deep thought as he listened to what the dark lord had to offer. Staring down into his glass, he said softly, "I'm just one being. With powers I don't even understand, or know the limits to." He looked up to meet Lucifer's eyes. "How am I to take on a whole race of demons?"

Lucifer smiled as he sat his goblet to the side. "With an army." They both vanished and appeared in a huge chamber near the gates of Hell. Inside were various humans and other kinds. All looked confused to be there but all held a certain malicious air about them.

It didn't take Bounce long to realize some wore prison garb, others had stab wounds in their clothes, ink on their faces. Some wore the armor of Spartans while others wore nothing more than a loincloth. "Murderers? Killers?" He faced Lucifer confused. "This is an army? These are criminals. They are not soldiers."

Lucifer smirked and gave a shrug, "What did you think I could offer from hell? Cherubs and fluffy puppies? This is what you get. But I can assure you, they are all skilled and deadly. And they have a reason to do whatever they are told to do."

Bounce ran a hand over his freshly sheared scalp as he looked at the rag-tag but pissed off ruffians. "And what is that?"

Lucifer held his hand out, palm up as if presenting a prize. "You hold the future of their souls. In pawn, we shall say. And they get a second chance to redeem their miserable existence and live again. And if they do it well, when you feel they have done their jobs, they can live again and have a chance at going to Heaven instead of," smiling as he did a play of words he was apparently quite proud of, "a bounce back to hell from you. No more second chance and I will make sure their hell fires burn hotter than they do now. You can lead them. Of this I have no doubt."

Bounce looked from the dark lord to his new "army", unsure why the devil had such faith. "Fine. Then let's get started."

CHAPTER TWELVE

1979

She was always running late. She tried to set alarms (she had bought two of the new digital alarm clocks, that didn't work to get her awake either) and as always she was late getting to her class. The irony wasn't lost on the fact that the students that rushed, just as late as she was would get tardy slips from her. It seemed almost comical as they wanted to say "you're never on time either" but didn't dare.

This morning she was late because she was out of coffee, and a third-grade teacher without coffee was most likely the most dangerous thing to be found when enclosed in a room with young minds looking to learn. Standing in the check-out line of the convenience store along with people getting gas, candy bars and pops, she wished someone would just open a store just for coffee. If they did? She would just live there.

Paying for the cup of coffee, she all but ran out of the store the one block to the school, already hearing the bell letting the student know class time had arrived, even from here. If she was lucky, Tanya would make it to her job just as the tardy bell rang.

Tanya was never lucky.

Hot coffee splashing all over him was not the way he wanted to start out the morning, and Bounce went to rip into the carrier of coffee until he met beautiful green eyes. His mouth was open, ready to slay with a string of colorful words but nothing sounded from his lips. The woman was short but tiny, with a knitted cap pulled over unruly brown hair. Her eyes looked too big for her face, but he thought they were perfect as they sat over a button nose and lips formed in the shape of an "O" that she had just ran into him.

And he was now wearing her coffee all over his Fleetwood Mac t-shirt. His new, signed by the band, Fleetwood Mac t-shirt. Some day that band would be considered classic and this shirt would be worth something. That is, if it now wouldn't be sporting a big brown stain.

"Oh, my gosh. I am so sorry." She frantically tried to wipe at the coffee with her gloved hand, her breath misting in the chilly San Francisco morning. Now her yellow gloves at least matched his shirt—coffee colored. "I didn't even see you there!" She looked up and she blinked. "How I could not see you is just mind boggling. I mean you're huge."

Her eyes went wide with what she said as she stepped back, a blush spreading on her cheeks. The man was indeed huge. Tall, muscled and gorgeous. Even through her gloves she could feel the ripples of muscle beneath his t-shirt and he towered over her. Every bit almost seven-feet and as beautiful as any Calvin Klein underwear model. Which just led Tanya's eyes down to where such underwear would be worn and realized she was staring at, well, that too. So, huge was an allover package deal with tall and coffee drenched. Cue blush darkening even more. "I guess, you don't need your coffee now?" She gave a sheepish smile as she turned her cup over to let the last drop splatter on the ground. "Glad I could help?"

A smile twitched his lips as he looked from her to his shirt, saying amused, "I don't drink coffee."

Tanya winced and bit her bottom lip, of course his voice would be sexy and exotic, why not totally make her look foolish to most likely the most perfect and straight male in San Francisco. "Well, I do." She put her hands over her mouth to hold back a laugh, "Quite obviously." The tardy bell rang and she tossed the cup. "But guess I won't be today. Sorry again!"

She took off running and Bounce yelled to her retreating back, "Wait, what's your name?"

Tanya turned to run backwards and responded, "Tanya Bishop." And of course, she then tripped over a crack in the sidewalk to land on her ass.

Bounce ran over to her and knelt beside her, trying not to laugh at the expression on her face sporting a blush that was even darker than the one earlier when she seemed fascinated with the fly on his Jordace jeans. "Are you okay?"

"Shoot!" If a person could die of embarrassment, she would love to be that person as she looked up at him. "I just should not have gotten out of bed." She went to stand and immediately let out a sound of pain as she put weight on her ankle. "Oh great. This is what I get for not doing my grocery shopping."

Bounce put a hand on her elbow to help her stand and then to steady as she hopped on one foot. She didn't seem to weigh anything as he wrapped an arm around her waist. "Here, let me help you." He waited until she put an arm across his shoulders, having to bend way down for her to do so. "This won't work."

Before she could say she didn't need any help, he was swinging her up off her feet to cradle in his arms. Oh gosh, if she thought he felt fine through her gloves, she had been totally misled. The body that pressed against her side as he carried her, along with the strong arms that held her were a big "there is so much more than what you're feeling" sensation of before. Like a lot more.

"Where were you going?" Tanya looked up as the deep, sensual voice said something and wanted to hide her face in his chest, which would most likely make things even more embarrassing. "To the school, yes?" The most beautiful grey eyes coming down to meet hers. Huh, she could have sworn they were blue before.

When she realized he had made the connection of the bell ringing and her rushing, she panicked. "No, no. We need to walk the other way." She pointed behind them, because they were walking straight to the school she taught in, and several of her fellow gossiping teachers were standing in front of the building. About that death by embarrassment... now would be good. Not too bad of a way to go, in the arms of a strong, sexy, beautiful stranger. Better than dying alone with my ice cream and a dozen cats. Well, I'll need to get cats first. Got the ice cream covered.

Tanya pulled her cap over her face as her rescuer reached the front walk of the school to say to the gawking women. "Hello, I believe she has injured her ankle."

Tanya peeked out from under her cap and swallowed, squeaking out, "I fell. I was almost on time?" Both women gave her a smirk and then flashed her rescuer bright, flirtatious smiles as they showed him the way up to the office, as he refused to put her down.

    And just to add to her "un-luck", all her students were looking out the door as they passed, each one giggling and whispering behind her hand.

    Just great—and she without coffee.

CHAPTER THIRTEEN

Lessons

"So, you're a teacher?" Bounce was looking at the child drawn pictures she had framed on the wall, along with photos of her standing with students, all smiling. He glanced back at Tanya as she hobbled her way to the couch, refusing to let him help, even though the doctor at the ER said her ankle was severely sprained. He found her stubbornness adorable as well as amusing as well as her disdain that he made it obvious he did so. She had tried to stop him from taking her to the emergency room, had told him to leave as they x-rayed her ankle and then stated she could catch a cab to her apartment. None of it had worked and she had even accused him of being deaf and not hearing her. It was the most pleasant morning he could remember ever having and that seemed to peeve her as well.

"Third through fifth grade. It's all I ever wanted to do growing up." She dropped down rather ungracefully on the couch to sit as she lifted her bandaged leg up to the coffee table. He sat on the arm of the couch opposite of her and smiled, listening as she explained. She had the most enchanting voice— something between a sing-song and a cartoon. It too amused him.

"Were your parents teachers?" He walked over to place a pillow under her ankle and glanced back at her gasp, "Did that hurt? Sorry."

Tanya shook her head fast, licking her bottom lip. It didn't hurt at all, in fact, when his fingers brushed her bare skin above the bandage, she felt a thrill. That was stupid, must be the pain meds she thought as she replied, "No. It didn't hurt. You're fine." *Super, eat him up with a biscuit, fine.*

Bounce couldn't help but smile at hearing her thoughts as he turned to sit once more. "So, your parents, Tanya, were they teachers?"

Tanya blinked and then remembered he had asked that before and she shrugged, reaching out to fidget with the bandage at her ankle. "I wouldn't know. I was orphaned pretty young and grew up with a nice couple as foster parents. But Ted was a professor, retired. He did make me love books and reading. I guess that contributed to my want to teach others to love words." *God, I miss them. Bet Ted would find all of this hilarious. Tanya, he's a stranger, be careful girl. Ted, just look at this guy. Me wanna look more.*

He watched the emotions that moved across her face as she spoke—sorrow when speaking of her parents but a fondness of her foster parents, and one again her thoughts told him more perhaps than she wanted him to know. "What happened to your foster parents?" He moved to sit on the end of the couch, turning to face her as he leaned back. She looked at him in surprise and he said softly, "Your tone, you said was. I'm good at reading people, it's a gift." He gave her a gentle smile and she sighed.

"They both were elderly when they became my foster parents. If they had been younger, they would have adopted me. But they both passed away when I was seventeen. He had a stroke and she, I feel, followed with a broken heart. They said it was a heart attack, but she was just so lost without him. I was old enough then to be on my own, so with the money, which wasn't much, they left me, I went to school and now, ten years later, I'm a teacher." She smiled and looked down, "I'd like to think I made them proud."

"I bet they are." He circled a hand and got up to refill her tea glass and his own, continuing as he reached her small kitchen. "I believe people we care about continue to be a part of us. As long as we go on, so do they." He came back and handed her the glass and sat back down. "So, your parents? You said you were orphaned young."

Tanya had no idea why this man seemed to be able to get her to talk. She was an introvert by nature yet something about this guy made it seem easy to talk. But when he asked about her parents, she shook her head and took a drink of tea to hide her anxiety of the subject. "Enough about me. Tell me about you. Do you often save clumsy damsel teachers in distress and get covered in coffee?" She smiled as she sat down her glass. Lucky coffee. Very lucky coffee, she thought as her eyes went to the now very dried and set in coffee stain on his shirt over that massive chest.

Bounce shrugged and draped an arm on the back of the couch, kicking up his high top Keds to rest on the coffee table next to her tiny foot. "Not much to say. I never knew my parents as I was abandoned early on. Grew up and came into some money and bought a club in the Tenderloin district. As far as my saving damsel teachers," smiling a wide smile, but careful not to show his fangs, "you would be my first. That makes you special."

Tanya giggled and pointed to his t-shirt. "I am sorry about that. I so wanted to go to that concert, but they were all out of tickets in hours. Bet it rocked."

Bounce looked down at his shirt and nodded. "It was incredible. My club helped sponsor the show, so I got to go backstage and got it autographed. I'm betting they will be a mega-band in a matter of months." He pulled the shirt away from his chest with his fingers, saying in amusement, "You must like a lot of sugar in your coffee, this is sticky." He glanced up at her. "Mind if I change? I have extras in my car." His car was a supped-up VW Thing painted in dark purple and black and when Tanya saw it, she was in awe. It was by far the coolest car she had ever seen.

Tanya pointed to the hall closet in her small apartment, "Actually, you can change into one of my ex- roomie's t-shirts. He was a big guy so they might fit you. Or," not wanting to admit she was enjoying his company and didn't want it to end even for him to go the half-block to his car, "you can get your own shirt." She bit her bottom lip with a grin and looked down at her glass. Smooth Tanya. Be a dork why don't you? Maybe you'll get lucky and he'll just strip..."Oh my god..."

Bounce had heard her thoughts and it was just too good to pass up. He was already on his feet, jacket off and tugging his shirt over his head. Tossing it to the floor, he pointed down her hall, "This way?"

Tanya just nodded, her jaw hanging so low she was surprised it didn't fall off. The man was the most perfect example of male she had ever seen. Chiseled chest and torso, with muscled arms corded with strength and over his heart was a strange symbol tattooed, done in black. A symbol that Tanya had seen around town, but never knew what it meant. Twisting to watch him walk away, she saw his back was just as impressive and his ass—did the man have any flaws physically? That was when she noticed he had ink also on his back. Not that strange but she could tell it was there to hide scars. Really big ones that went at an upward angle over each shoulder blade. The ink was tribal in nature, but was in inked with flames to cover the scars. Watching him come back, tugging on a vintage Led Zeppelin shirt, she looked down with a frown to hide that she had been looking.

"So, uh. I haven't even asked your name. And isn't there a girl or uh," heck, this was San Francisco after all, "a guy that's probably wondering where you are? I think it's great you helped me and all, but no way you didn't have other things you might like to be doing."

He lifted his wrist to look at his watch and winced, not realizing the day had gotten so late. He couldn't remember the last time he had just kicked back and relaxed. He looked up at Tanya and knew he would have to give her all the credit for she was simply so adorably engaging. "You can call me Bounce. And yeah, you're right; I do have things to do." He saw her face and smiled. "But there is no girl. And guy? No. I'm not gay if that's what you're wondering. I'm one of those rare, single, heterosexual San Fran males you've heard rumors about. They do exist. Still not sure about unicorns though. But I'll let you know." He then teased her with a wink.

Tanya got to her feet gingerly and grinned. "Well, at least I have one myth marked off my list of impossibilities." She pointed to the door and then back and then just decided to put her hands away behind her back before she started doing some weird "will you call me charades" with them. "Thanks for today. It was very nice of you." She met his eyes and once again, could have sworn they were a different color earlier, but not the deep green they were now. "Bounce." She wrinkled her nose and pursed her lips. "That's a very strange name."

Bounce had heard that millions of times over the centuries, but for some reason he didn't completely understand, he wished he had a real name to give to this girl. He smiled, "I said you could call me that. Everyone else does, never said it was my name." He looked down to see her putting some weight on her foot and pulled his jacket off the couch and slipped it on. "Make sure you take it easy, Tanya. And it was nice meeting you. I'll have this returned." Pointed to the t-shirt he wore as he picked up his own. "Along with some coffee so you don't harm any future heroes not in the saving teachers game."

Tanya blushed slightly as she said with a smile. "Thank you, Bounce."

Bounce returned the smile and bent down low to say softly in her ear, "No. Thank you, Tanya. Very much." Then just like that, he was heading out her door, closing it behind him.

Tanya dropped back down to sit on the couch and it was strange. Her cozy apartment seemed so much smaller and darker without Bounce in it. It was odd, she barely knew the man but there was just something about him. And she missed it....and him.

"Stop it, Tanya. No more cheesy romances for you." She sighed and then smacked her hands over her face. "And maybe I need to buy those cats."

CHAPTER FOURTEEN

Wishful Thinking

Lachesis stared down at the water in the Well of Souls, her mind not on the task at hand one bit. Her sisters had just left and even commented on her silence. Giving up trying to make her talk and leaving, she did what she did whenever granted time alone.

"Show me."

Slowly the water swirled and soon an image appeared on the surface of the water. She had no idea how it could appear since she had hidden Mali's thread—perhaps it was because they had been physically linked from making love, or perhaps the fact that the thread was still part of the well, albeit hidden beyond even her reach, but whenever she asked, she was shown what she sought. She had been doing this for centuries and she kept lying to herself when believed that it was only to check on his well-being. To make sure no one had learned all she had taken so many measures to hide.

The night after she had visited him in hell was still as if it had happened a few hours ago. She had somehow made her way back to Mount Olympus after her conversation with Lucifer, assured by the dark lord that the man she loved would be protected. She had been sobbing when she collapsed in the temple of her great-great aunt Mnemosyne, the goddess of memory, crying out to her for help.

"What is it, child? What has you so rendered emotionally?

Lachesis reached out to grasp her aunt's robe, dropping her head to plead. "I wish to forget. I need to forget. To never remember again. Can you help me?"

Mnemosyne knelt down to cup her face, giving her an understanding look, "You wish to forget love? I can tell from your pain. Oh my child, that is the hardest of memories to erase. Or forget. Are you sure?"

Lachesis had to do whatever she needed to do to make sure Mali's true identity was never learned by those who would use him, destroy him and the world. She met her aunt's eyes and nodded, "I want to keep my memories of his time with me. But I need to forget what came before. And," she hesitated revealing all, afraid her sisters would find out what she did and search for the thread, "forget what I did to protect him and how."

Mnemosyne's brow furrowed in concern as she said softly, brushing her god niece's tears away with her fingers. "The past not yours is simple. But a task you have done? That, I cannot promise won't return when the time for it to be revealed is shown. Do you still wish this?"

Lachesis nodded. "Yes. Please. I want to stop this hurting."

Her aunt took her hand to stand with her and cupped her face. "Then we shall begin."

Lachesis was pulled back to the present by the sound of an exotic familiar voice. Looking down at the image in the well as she wiped tears away with the back of her hand, she smiled when Mali's face appeared. She knew he now went by the name of Bounce, which she found amusing but sad as well when she learned of the reason. Reaching out to touch the water, wishing it was he she was touching, she said softly, "Hello love." He was talking to someone and she widened her fingers touch on the surface of the water to expand the view.

"Who is that?" A young woman sat with Mali, smiling and then blushing as he spoke. Of course there would be a woman and she was glad. But as she watched, some strange fear crept up her spine, turning her blood chilled.

She could tell it was a human and not a supernatural being, but for some reason Lachesis knew this person would become crucial in Mali's life. And something would change.

And Lachesis could do nothing about it.

Bringing a hand up to her mouth, she looked away as a sob sounded. "Take it away. I don't want to see anymore." She stood as the image vanished. She had to stop doing this to herself. How was she ever going to get over him if she stalked him like some peeper into his life? Why did she still have such strong feelings for a man who she had not personally seen, touched or held in centuries? She hissed out in frustration, "Why can't I stop loving you!"

"Because love is like that, sister dear."

Lachesis whipped around to see the youngest fate, Clotho standing in the doorway. She had been so self- absorbed that her entrance had gone unnoticed. She wiped her tears, standing up straight to regain her composure. She rarely showed her more fragile side—a lesson learned the day Mali was thrown from her arms to die. "You have a terrible habit of eavesdropping sister."

Clotho gave a slight smile, brushing her blonde hair from her eyes to look at Lachesis. "I know, but some of my sisters don't share. It's the only way I have to find out how to help." She walked up and took her sister's hands in hers. "You still miss him? The beautiful unknown one?"

Lachesis cocked a brow, ready to deny and rebuff her sister's attempt at care but sighed as she looked down at their linked hands. Maybe it would be nice to share and get some insight from someone, anyone, at this point. "I do. It makes no sense. It seems like it's been forever."

Clotho sat, pulling Lachesis down with her. "Do you think you ever will?" She titled her head to smile as she crinkled her nose. "I don't think you do. You tried to save him." Her voice went kind and soft. "He was your first lover. Your first love. The touch of that on your heart never goes away. No matter how hard we try."

Lachesis realized that Clotho, like everyone else, thought Mali was dead, which gave her some comfort it was worth it. But then she realized her sister seemed to have more understanding than she was aware of and she met Clotho's eyes. "We try? Clo? You fell in love too? Who? When?"

Clotho looked away and smiled. "It doesn't matter, sister. I, like you, had to let them go. And still long for them and miss them and wish..." her words trailed off as she rose to her feet. "Enough. It is the way of our lives, is it not? To be without a mate. Only lovers to be used and shuffled away when their use is done." She straightened her robes and cleared her throat. "I can only say that if you think your lover was met with Zeus disapproval, mine most definitely would trump yours." She shrugged. "Why I shall never bring another lover to this place. It may be paradise but it is just a prison masquerading as one." She reached over to brush her fingers on Lachesis cheek. "It gets better. Or so I keep telling myself."

Lachesis wanted to ask her who and how. Clotho was the sweetest and gentlest of the two, but neither she nor Atropos thought she could hide anything, much less a lover that was more than just a toy. One that she had apparently been in love with.

But her sister was already to the door and then vanished before she could even ask.

CHAPTER FIFTEEN

Club Bounce

"**B**oss. I got the patrol roster as well as the alert reports for the last 24 hours. You want them now or later?"

Bounce looked up as one of his Breakers, the elite immortal fighters in his army, stepped in. Evan was the best and therefore Bounce trusted him with much. Part of that was the man acting as security head at the club. The club was just a front actually—dance floor on two levels, both with bars and Bounce's living space on the top floor. It was a great venue for moving the money and resources needed to fight the war as well as a hangout for those involved in it to get away and let loose.

Humans had no idea that they danced with immortal bad-asses and their human assistants called Relays, and didn't seem to care. Some humans were hired specifically to serve them, made aware of who and what they were so that they didn't freak when a Breaker showed his fangs or wanted sex beyond the "norm". They were paid well to keep the secret and the price of breaking that was far harsher than the rewards. "Yeah, put it down," waving a hand to the piles of papers and files on the corner of his desk, "there. Somewhere."

Evan snorted and popped a hip to sit on the opposite corner, dropping the reports, wondering when or if they would be looked at. Not that he cared.

His duty stopped when they hit that pile in that regards. "You okay? Seem real distracted the last few days."

Bounce sat back and tossed the file he was looking at down and regarded Evan. "How many women would you say you've had sex with?"

Evan smiled and brought his hand up to look at his fingers, eyes shifting as he did a mental count and then shrugged. "Not sure. Been decades of being this handsome so more than I can count. I'm a regular Dig Dug of passion. I just dig in and keep going. Why?" That was the big word Evan wondered about. Everyone knew that Bounce could have his pick—successful club owner that most thought was a super-model who had dozens of women each night propositioning him. But as far as Evan knew? None of them had been invited to the "friendly" bathrooms or service alley and definitely not a one had been to the third floor.

Bounce picked up that stupid Rubik's cube that was supposed to help him with stress. All it did was piss him off as he could never get all the colors lined up. Bad-ass, god, club owner, leader of a war...and a stupid block of stupid plastic squares with stupid colors was defeating him. Everyone thought it was amusing but each time they showed it, they got a full-fanged scowl from their usually easy going boss. Now they kept it well hidden, which included Evan who looked away to hide his grin. Narrowing his eyes, he threw the cube across the office, causing it to land on the well-worn couch that acted as his bed most nights. "I met someone."

Evan's brows went up and he laughed. "You meet dozens every night, boss. Dozens more that wished they could meet you. Not sure if I get what you're saying."

"I met someone I would like to know better." He met Evan's eyes and blew out a long breath, then smirked. "A human. One who knows nothing about any of this. The war, what I am, nothing. She didn't hit on me, throw herself at me," he smiled and said softly, "unless you count the coffee. It was refreshing."

"Getting coffee on you was refreshing? Maybe you need to change your shower habits."

Bounce flipped him off at that as he got to his feet. "No, she is different. Sweet and adorable. And so far from what I should be hooking up with." He leaned against the wall, crossing his arms and ankles to look down at the floor. "It's been a very long time since I've met someone I wanted to know more about. Spend more time with. And not worry about what it was going to cost me. But..." lifting his eyes to his friend, "to bring anyone into this insanity is not wise. She's an elementary school teacher." He snorted and looked back down at the floor, "and a clumsy, shy woman. This?" waved a hand around his office, "totally different from her world. And that's not even tossing in the supernatural and war parts into the intro."

Evan could see his boss' point. Club Bounce was the hip place to go if you wanted to party on the fringe. Being in the Tenderloin district, it was the hottest place to explore those dark desires you might not want anyone to know about. Hence the low lighting, the pounding bass line and private couches and corners. Breakers could find whatever they needed to make it through another day of being a hero and Relays could break free of the tight restraints and demands placed on them in helping in the war. Humans were allowed and never the wiser to what the Club truly was. Social get-away for battered warriors and their sidekicks.

"I see your point. We're not exactly PTA approved." Evan stood and picked up one of the club schedules from Bounce's desk. "Why don't you give her a VIP package?" Flipped the card over to show him. "The works. Have the car pick her up, give her a VIP table, everything. If she's cool at that, then maybe in time the rest she can handle. Or not. But you need to find out, right?"

Bounce took the schedule from his hand and scanned down the upcoming acts. His mind then went to what bands were in Tanya's "ex's" collection of rock bands and he smiled. "That's a really good idea. You're a very smart goomba."

Evan laughed. "And you're great, King Koopa. Can I go now?"

Bounce nodded and shoved him to the door, dismissing as he reached for his office phone. "Yeah please. I'm sure you'll need to start on your hair for tonight."

Evan left as the call was answered by the club's secretary, a muni relay by the name of Donna. "Yes sir?"

He looked at the schedule and said with a smile, "I need a VIP package delivered for the 19th. The works and as my personal special guest."

Tanya was doing her toenails when the doorbell rang, causing her to waddle with tissue shoved between her toes to the door. It had been two weeks since she had sprained her ankle so it was healed, but there wasn't a day that didn't go by when she wondered if she'd ever see Bounce again.

She opened the door to find one of the dozens of bike messengers of the city standing there holding out a huge dark purple foil-looking envelope. "You Tanya?"

Tanya looked down at the envelope with a nod, putting the bottle of polish in her teeth. "I am." The messenger handed her the delivery and then left, leaving her standing there. She looked down the hall and back before closing the door and waddling back to the couch. Setting the bottle on the table, she sat back to open the flap on the envelope and pulled out the contents.

"VIP?" There was a scrunchie that was utilized as a bracelet with a laminated card attached like a charm that said "VIP of Club Bounce." Her heart skipped a beat at just seeing his name, not even sure if the two were connected, but didn't he say he owned a club? She picked up the handwritten note and a smile spread across her face as she let out a squeal.

Tanya,

Sorry I'm just now contacting you. Been busier than Mario in a mushroom patch. I'd be very happy if you would be my guest at the upcoming Blondie concert. I can send a car and I promise you'll have a great time. I'll even have a sippy cup for your drinks. :)

Hoping to see you soon,
Bounce
P.S. - Thanks for loaning the shirt

She dumped out the rest of the contents and there was a card for the club with Bounce's name written on the back and the words "Guest of" along with the t-shirt she had loaned him, freshly laundered. She laughed as several packets of instant coffee slid out to the table. There was also a flyer for the concert that night. "Blondie? Never heard of them." But then again, books were her friend, not music. She jumped up and held it all to her chest, spinning around and doing a little dance. She didn't want to think that she may be a guest in a group of dozens of others of the same, for that would just crush her glee.

No, in her mind, this was all about just her. "I finally heard from him!" She jumped up and down in victory and then realized she spilled the polish all over the table by hitting it somehow. "Oh shoot!" She ran to grab some paper towels and noticed she had also ruined her pedicure. "Oh well, think I'll go get some purple polish." She giggled and spun around again.

She was going to see him again and that was all that mattered.

Tanya felt so out of her element. First she had missed the car by running late after shopping, having no idea what to wear which led to having to use the public bus to get here. Now, she was standing in a line waiting to get let into what looked like a huge old warehouse, except for the booming sound of Foreigner sounding through the metal and brick walls along with the crowd standing outside dressed from punk to prep standing with her.

She looked down at her jeans and tied up Jefferson Starship t-shirt along with ankle boots and decided this was the worst idea. All the girls in the line were talking about all the incredibly hot guys that waited inside and two had even got excited when they heard Bounce was in the club tonight. Like he was some rock star of something. She was turning to go and just send him a note saying she fell down getting ready, which he would most likely believe, rather than be the ugly duckling in a pond of perfect.

"You're VIP?"

She turned to see the larger than possible bouncer by the door and glanced at her wrist where the pass was looped. "Oh. Yeah. I am." Looked at it and then back at him. "Was it a mistake?"

The man grasped the small laminated badge and read it, his eyes going wide. "Oh, Bounce's personal VIP. You should have said something. Boss doesn't do that often. Come right in." The girls standing around her gawked, their jaws dropping as the bouncer came back to personally lead her inside. She smiled and held up her arm, saying a bit louder than needed, "Excuse me. Personal VIP of Bounce. You know, the owner...." The bouncer shook his head in amusement as he held the door open for her.

And it was a whole different world.

Bounce was standing at the second floor rail, looking down at a packed club. The band Blondie was starting to get some major radio time, so they had hit their limit pretty quick. The guys working the door had to play the shuffle out, shuffle in as each person came and went. All the tickets were sold out and the bar was flowing with liquor, the dance floor on both levels swaying with grinding bodies and the bribe to the fire marshal guy paid. Even that guy was dancing with a beautiful girl below.

"She wasn't there, Boss."

He glanced over at Evan and frowned. "Thanks." Turning to face the second floor, his eyes scanned the occupants and felt eased that nothing too deadly graced them tonight. The bonus of having Breakers and Wires (the enforcers) here to party was that they, just like he, could sense Eaters and clear them out pretty quick with no humans the wiser. Tonight there were the usual immortals, demons and humans, none to be given the boot or watched. Lowering his head, he sighed deep as he looked at the tip of his Michael Jordan high tops. Tanya hadn't showed.

He didn't know why he was surprised—he was pretty sure the young woman wasn't a clubber and if she was smart, which he was confident she was, she would have checked into what type of club she was going to. Hell, just being in the Tenderloin district emphasized it was most likely not her type of venue. Blowing a frustrated breath of his nose, he pushed off to head upstairs, not in the mood at all for the energy the club had to offer tonight.

"Dance with us!" Before he could stop, two bold young women had grabbed his arms to pull them all to the dance floor. He gave each a polite smile; eyes going to the stairs of his escape plan as he moved to the motion of the song letting them try their best to entice him with their bodies grinding on his.

Tanya wandered as much as she could with a drink, untouched, in her hand to see all the club had to offer. Beautiful people gyrated and moved on the dance floor and she did her best not to look into the darkened corners where other bodies were doing gyrations of a different kind. She had been bumped into, glared at and more than once been grabbed in an effort to have her "loosen up, baby" by some male, and a few females. As she was making her way up the stairs, finding more people "loosening" up sitting there, she froze when she reached the second floor landing.

She couldn't help but not see immediately the beautiful man on the dance floor being seduced by two attractive females. One was rubbing her butt all over his front while the other was rubbing her front all over his butt. She blinked as Bounce danced along, his eyes going upward and back, not seeing her.

She turned to look where his gaze had switched too and saw the sign at the top of those stairs that said- "No Admittance, Private". Oh, that's right, he lived here too. Seeing he had already found his VIPs for the night and most likely would be escorting them upstairs, she turned and started to run down the stairs.

Bounce sensed rather than saw Tanya fleeing down the stairs, so he turned to see her heading out of the club in a frenzied pace. Having to pry the two females off of him, he went running after her, catching her in the middle of the downstairs dance floor. "Hey! Where are you going?"

Tanya didn't know why she was angry. Or if she was hurt—maybe both. But as soon as she heard his voice behind her, she threw her drink at him, literally, glass and all in his face. The glass hit him right between the eyes with a loud thud as the liquid, some pink concoction, splashed all over his shirt. She yanked her arm away from his grasp during his shocked pause and ran towards the door. "Stay away from me! Go back to your playthings upstairs!"

The dancers around them backed up, as if expecting the club owner to explode, but all Bounce did was blink and wipe the drink from his eyes. The DJ had even stopped playing music, until Bounce gave him a raised brow scowl, and it started up again. Making his way through the resuming bodies moving to the music, he caught up once again with Tanya before she got to the exit. "Wait. Let me explain."

Tanya whipped around and pointed a finger up at his face, angrily trying to brush her wild hair from her face with her other hand. "First you invite me then I have to see you all over not one, but two floozies? Are they VIPs too?" She let out a growl as she wrenched the VIP badge off her wrist to throw that too in his face. "What do you do? Gather them all here in a herd and see which one you want to ride first? God! I'm such an idiot."

Bounce would had been greatly amused by her tirade until he realized she was truly upset and that, he didn't like. "Hey, first, I was dancing. I was barely doing that. I don't even know who those women are. Look around you, Tanya, it's a dance club. Dancing is what we do here." He had caught her badge and stepped up to sweep her hair up in his hands, pulling it away from her flushed face to bundle it behind her, placing it in a ponytail with the scrunchie. "I didn't think you were coming. The car I sent said you weren't home." He dropped his hands and gave her a smile. "I would have much rather danced with you."

Tanya felt her anger melting under the brightness of that smile but she put her chin up in defiance of that to say firmly, "I was late. I had to shop. I'm always late." Her eyes went down to his shirt and she winced, looking up at the matching pink, reddish spot between his eyes. "I did it again. All your clothes are doomed."

He laughed and looked down, once again chest covered in a liquid tossed from her hand. "Well, they wash." He looked around the club and back down at her, so glad to see her. Happy, which was something he didn't feel often. "Do you want to talk? Away from all this? I was so excited to have you come experience the club, a part of my world, but now," bringing a hand up to cup her cheek, "all I want is to have you all to myself."

Tanya's heart did a weird beat at his touch and another one at his words. She smiled and gave him a nod as she said in a whisper, "I'd love that, actually."

CHAPTER SIXTEEN

So, this is...

"**O**h come on, tell me, why do you go by Bounce?"

They were sitting on the couch in his office, the loud pulse of the club still heard but far away down the long staff hallway. He sat on the opposite end from her, his elbow on the back as his head rested on his palm. He was completely, totally smitten with this adorable woman sitting in front of him. He now knew she was twenty-six years old, had no family and completely loved her job. And was always late and had a thing for never seeing movies that were made from books. He gave her another easy smile and said with a shrug, "I don't know my given name. So I've gone by Bounce for so long, that's what I know. And what I like." He moved his hand to rest on the couch cushion between them, just a hair away from her fingers. He looked down and noticed the dark purple nail polish and smiled as he noticed her suede ankle boots matched. "So, you went shopping? For me?" tapped one of her nails, "and painted your nails my favorite color."

Tanya blushed a bit and held up a leg, the one that previously he had seen bandaged up, to admire her boots. "Oh, is this your favorite color? I didn't even know that." Lie! You so did notice. It was on his car and the card and everything. Guy likes dark purple and is straight? How rare is that?

Bounce couldn't help but smile once more at hearing her thoughts as he got up to get them both a soda out of the fridge.

Tanya watched him move and it was like watching some predatory creature of fantasy when he was in motion. All his muscles seemed to flow and curve to almost make it look like the man was doing some sensual salsa when just doing the simple act of walking. *God, I wonder what he'd be like during sex? No! Stop that Tanya, bad teacher, bad, bad.*

Bounce was taking a drink of his soda when that thought crossed through Tanya's mind to his, and he choked on the bubbly liquid, coughing hard. Tanya was on her feet, running over to rub his back, alarmed at his distress. He waved her off, holding out a soda for her to take and gave her a grin as he regained his composure. "Sorry, swallowed too fast. It was bad soda, bad, bad."

Tanya narrowed her eyes and tilted her head, but then wrote it off as coincidence as they made their way back to the couch. She sat back down, folding her legs under her as she laid her head on the back of the couch. "So," circling her fingers on the space between them, "I'm guessing being a club owner of a place like this gets you uh, lots of uh, well, uh..." she was unsure how to word it as her nose crinkled in thought.

"Playthings?" He couldn't help it. She was even more adorable when she was unsure.

Tanya blushed and let out a soft giggle. "Oh. That was so wrong of me. I'm sorry. But basically, yes." She lifted her eyes to his to say softly, "Dates. Girlfriends. Uh, overnight stays."

He looked down to take her hand in his on the cushion between them, his long lashes hiding his eyes as he replied low, "No. Actually. They try but I've never been," he lifted his eyes to hers then and she was once again struck how the shade had to be changing, for they were going almost to a soft purple now, "interested."

She let out a soft "oh" and before she could say more he had moved forward to kiss her. She didn't mind as his strong arms went around her, his lips softer than she could have ever imagined, his muscles growing taut under her touch as she splayed her hands on his chest. The kiss was unbelievably gentle, which surprised her considering the hungry and deadly air that seemed to have bloomed just seconds before his mouth had claimed hers.

Tanya was no virgin, but she could count the boyfriends on one hand and the lovers on two fingers. But none of them, heck, all of them combined, didn't stir the desire as this man did with that one kiss. Soon, she was kissing him back, their tongues dancing as bodies of others did beyond this room. His hands seem to be everywhere, which was also fine with her, since hers were all over him.

Shirts hit the floor, purple boots went flying across the room, landing somewhere in a heap, followed by pants and other articles of dress.

Bounce was above her, bare skin to bare skin, kissing her face, neck and breasts and Tanya couldn't breathe with the emotions of it all. She braced her hands on his shoulders, pushing him up a bit to meet his eyes, now a dark purple. She tried to form thoughts as she gasped out, "Please say I'm not a plaything."

Bounce looked into her eyes, bringing a hand up to cup her chin, kissing her softly and then moving his head to whisper in her ear, "No. Playthings are never allowed in my heart." He lifted his head to once again to meet her eyes, his voice so painfully sincere as he said words he never thought he's say, "Because that's where you are."

And with that, Tanya was completely, totally, no-going-back, lost.

"So," she asked, with Bounce laying with his head on her stomach, their sweaty limbs tangled as they cooled down from making love right there in his office, "you won't tell me your name. Because you don't have one. And I know you own a club and girls want in your under-roos," loving the chuckle that rumbled in his chest against her legs, "so how old are you?"

Bounce frowned a bit at that and lifted his head to rest his chin on her bellybutton. "Thirty-two." It was a bold lie but how was he going to tell her he was a god and thousands of years old? That was not listed in the "how to date your way to love if you're an immortal unknown god" handbook. If such a thing even existed. Her brow creased, that cute nose crinkling once more as she soaked that in with a nod.

"And have you lived in San Fran your whole life?"

He put his cheek back on her belly as he shook his head to answer. "No. I've only lived here for about 10 years. When I bought the club. Before that I just traveled all over, a bit of an explorer if you will." Or he could have just said he went all over the world seeking the main entry point of the demons trying to destroy mankind only to find it right here under the Bridge in the bay. Nope, probably best to keep that to himself now too.

"Does that mean you're rich?" She bit her bottom lip with her teeth when she realized how that must have sounded as he lifted his head to look up at her.

He smiled as he said softly, moving up to tease her breast again, "Yes. I am. Are you going to blackmail me? If so, I believe I should have my way with you a dozen or more times to make it worth the crime. We'll call it punishment."

Tanya's mind started losing the ability to form thoughts as his lips captured her nipple, her teeth biting her bottom lip with a groan as his hands started helping his mouth to torture her lower. "Bounce. I want to know about you. Learn about you." As much as she regretted it, she gently grasped his soft hair, to pull his head up. "I need to know about you."

Bounce sighed and dropped his head down to say softly, "I don't share easily. I've already told you more than I have told anyone. Well, with the exception of one other person, but she's been gone from my life for a very long time." He lifted his head and moved up more so their faces were just inches apart to look into her eyes. "Ask me. I'll answer. I trust you."

Tanya had no idea why such simple words as "I trust you" made her feel so incredibly special and valuable. As his eyes searched hers, she made a point of focusing on their color, but they remained a soft green. "Your eyes. Why do they change?"

He swallowed and moved to sit up, blowing out a breath of nervousness, running his fingers through his hair. So, expose her to his world, he did tell her to ask after all. Was he ready for this? He looked at her and knew, maybe not, but he wanted her in it, so it was time to talk about it. "It's an anomaly. A one-of-a-kind one. I've never seen or heard anyone else having them. All eyes change."

He glanced at her and said softly, as he ran a hand along her leg; pausing at a scar she had on her knee, focusing on that, "Sadness, happiness is all reflected in our eyes. They grow brighter in happiness or dull in pain." He glanced back at her, saying with a shrug, "Mine just do it to a greater degree, depending on my mood." He looked across the room. "I usually control it. But I guess with you, I can't." He swallowed and looked down. "Or I don't want to."

Tanya sat up, cupping his face to turn it towards her as she smiled, saying softly, "They're beautiful. I like that you feel you can show me all the colors of your emotions. I will so make a cheat sheet." She laughed softly and kissed him. "That's all for today."

She stood up and he looked at her in confusion. "All? For today?" She was slipping his shirt on and he thought that was the most beautiful sight in the world. And a real turn-on as his flesh started to harden at just the sight.

"Well, I'm a teacher. I believe in taking it slow on my students. Learning as we go. And you did good. You shared," she got a wicked look on her face, "a lot. In all kinds of ways," bringing a finger up to her matching devious smile to bite her nail," so, tomorrow we'll do more lessons. In all kinds of ways."

Bounce laughed, putting his hands on her hips to pull her back down, letting her straddle his lap. He kissed her, winding his fingers in her hair as he said softly, "Are you sure you want to learn it all?"

Tanya thought about that as she draped her arms on his shoulders, her fingers coming up to play with the hair at the nape of his neck. "I do. I promise. I really do. If you'll let me."

Bounce stared the sweetest, kindest, most adorable woman he had ever met and thought about what she said. He looked down, running his hands along her thighs. It was a risk, a huge one that not only impacted him on a deep personal level but the war as well. A war they had kept hidden from humanity beyond those involved with it. His brow creased and he licked suddenly dry lips. Blowing out a breath that seemed to take forever, he lifted his eyes as they phased into the deepest evergreen and nodded. "I will. I'll let you. Just don't break my heart. You're the first one I've ever let in it."

Tanya's eyes filled with tears the ragged emotion in his voice as she brought her hands forward to cup his face, watching as his eyes changed into such a beautiful color. Whispered as she brought her lips to his, "Green means love. Affection. It's now my color. How could I break your heart when I have my own color?"

Then her lips claimed his and Bounce was just as lost as she.

CHAPTER SEVENTEEN

One Year Later

"I do not see your fascination with that damn thing." Bounce had his face buried against Tanya's neck as she sat in his lap, curled up despite her huge baby bump. A bump that contained their daughter. His hand rested there, loving the pure sweet innocent light energy that pulsed through their child. Her pregnancy had been so easy and perfect that at times he was overwhelmed with a sense of blessing, not sure who to thank for it. Tanya had learned she was pregnant just three months into their relationship and in that time had learned all there was to know about him.

He had been amazed how accepting she was, even though with each revelation she did the cutest "no way" with each one. So much so, he would laugh and have to rephrase her, only for her to correct his grammar. It was pure bliss sharing all that his life involved with someone. When she learned of her pregnancy, she had given up her job at the school and he had demanded she moved into his loft on the top floor of the club and since then he had spoiled and waited on her. Never had a pregnant woman been so pampered. Except for her latest hobby.

"I think it's wonderful." She laughed softly as she moved the Rubik's Cube's colored squares around, in yet another effort to solve it—having lost count how many attempts that had been. Bounce had pulled it from her hands almost the same count for he hated the thing. "You're telling me, almighty, old as air god of unknown powers and beautiful, kaleidoscope eyeballs that you've never been able to solve it?" She crinkled her nose to pull back to look at him, mocking shock on her face. "Can't you do some special Jedi mind trick thingy to make it be solved? I'm starting to rethink loving you, if you don't have those powers."

Bounce smirked and grumbled an amused, "ha-ha" before pulling it once again from her fingers and tossing it over his shoulder to land on the couch in the office. The same couch she had found it in one night when they were making out months ago, before he moved back to kissing and teasing her neck.

"That's why I can never solve it. You're always taking it away!" Tanya's breath was already turning into gasps as Bounce's hand explored her breasts, the other moving up her leg as his mouth made her forget how to think. "You're just afraid I'll show you up. Right?" She smiled as she felt his mouth still.

Bounce lifted his head once more, his eyes narrowing and she ducked her head down to see his eyes and smiled, laughing as he smirked. "Ah ha! Still green, you're not really angry."

Yeah, Tanya had learned his colors and it made it useless to even try to pull anything over on her. He had no idea why he was unable to control their phasing around her, but had given up trying weeks after they had fallen in love. But his eyes, just as everything else she had learned, she had kept secret between them. The Breakers all knew she was aware of their world and they adored her as well. Tanya had found the family she had never had, and he found the love he always needed. He had stopped worrying about any love or relationships he may have had before he washed up on that beach eons ago as well as the love he could have had with Lachesis, though the goddess came up to his mind often. He had never told Tanya about her or what had happened as it was still a sore spot—even after all this time. He was unsure why.

Suddenly Tanya let out a squeal and he looked down at her stomach, saying with a smile, "She's kicking." He immediately moved her out of his lap carefully before he dropped down to his knees and placed his cheek on her belly. Tanya brought a hand down to brush her fingers through his hair as he whispered, "Hello little one. It's me, your daddy. I can't wait to meet you." His eyes went to the calendar and he realized Tanya's due date was just two weeks away. He had already secured the best Grid physicians as well as midwives to be in the VIP suite at the hospital, as the administrator was also a Muni Relay who had that civilian job. Their daughter kicked again as if she heard him and he raised his t-shirt, which was the only items of clothes Tanya seemed to want to wear, and kissed her outie bellybutton or her "poke when it's done" button, as Tanya called it. He lifted his eyes to hers and said softly, choked up with emotion, "Marry me."

Tanya's breath caught as her mouth came open, but no sound was issued. She looked into those beautiful eyes and they were the darkest green she had ever seen. All beings should be as open with their emotions as this god she loved more than life itself as he whispered his love to their child and then, asked her the biggest question a woman in love could be asked. She bit her bottom lip, afraid that she was dreaming and perhaps this was that pivotal moment when one found out it was all just a dream and she would wake up, having dozed off in class or something.

"Are you sure?" she whispered as he got to his feet, to look down at her, taking her hands in his. "I don't want you asking just because you knocked me up. Or just because you think you have to. I'm fine with this, what we have Bounce. Always. And forever. I don't care how you love me just that you do."

Bounce smiled as he brushed her hair back, thumbs caressing her checks and asked once more, "Will you marry me?"

She smiled and let out a loud squeal as she threw her arms around him and held him as close as her big belly would let her. "Yes. Yes. Yes. If you promise me one thing," she pulled back to meet his eyes with a very serious look, "you never throw the cube of wonderfulness from my hands again. It's a deal breaker."

He laughed, kissing her before he said against her lips, "I hereby swear to never throw that damn cube again. Ever."

"Sister?"

Lachesis was sitting in the courtyard in the center of the Fate's temple when she heard her sister, Clotho speak. Looking over at her, she gave her a slight smile as her sister walked over. "Clotho. It's nice to see you. Back from earth."

Clotho sat across from her and clasped her hands in her lap, a worrisome look on her face before she nodded. "Yes. A birth thread beckoned me." She met Lacy's eyes and said softly, afraid someone would hear them, even here. "It's the Unknown's child."

Lachesis sat forward in shock, not sure if she had heard her sister correctly. "You knew? All this time?" Although she had forced herself to stop checking on Mali so often, surely she would have sensed this? Something? She got to her feet to pace, wringing her robe in her fingers as she moved. "A child? A woman is having his child?"

Clotho rose as well to walk over to her, gently touching her arm. "Yes. But I didn't tell father or anyone. I know you love him still and wished to protect him. He's been with a woman. A human woman, for a year now. They seem very happy. I only know because the thread showed me her parents. They're having a girl. And sooner than he thinks. It's mere hours before the birth, which is why the thread beckoned me to return."

Lachesis had never told a soul where Mali's thread was hidden, for she herself didn't follow its path. But she knew one thing...this child's birth was the most important thing to happen in Mali's life. Her gift to him for all they had shared so long ago. She clasped Clotho's hands in hers and said with a smile, "I'm going to earth. I have to be there."

Clotho gave her a look of alarm, pleading, "Lachesis! He's happy! In love! Why must you go?" Lachesis smiled and said as she ran to get ready, "I know! But I have to see that it was all worth it!"

The nightclub had been shut down to the public for the night as it was hosting a private party. A party that also included the wedding of its owner Bounce to the woman he loved, Tanya. All the Breakers as well as Relays closest to Bounce were present. Evan was his best man and Tanya had chosen the mid-wife that she had become close to,

Linda Devenmore as her maid of honor, who was present with her husband and their infant son. They were all drinking and eating the tons of food made by all the women as well as laughing how they never thought their boss was going to get married.

Bounce was nervously trying to put on a tie. That went with a tuxedo. But he had drawn the line at wearing the stiff uncomfortable loafers, so his new Michael Jordan high-tops would have to work. Fighting once more with the silk tie, he gave up and threw it across the room. He had a bad habit of that as Tanya was always showing him items she found where, like behind the couch, under the desk, in the sink or just lying in the floor. It was a habit he had to stop himself from doing as he glanced at the Rubik's Cube setting on his desk. She was so close to solving it...she had woke him up at 5am to show him how in just two more moves, it would be done. He had stopped her and said they should do the last move when the baby was born—and then let their daughter start as soon as she was able to do it, with her mommy helping of course. Tanya had thought that was a wonderful idea, so the cube now rested on a stand on his desk, awaiting one turn after they married and the final turn when their child was born.

He still hated the damn thing.

"Boss? It's time." Evan stuck his head in the door and grinned at the open collar of Bounce's dark purple shirt. "I can't believe she chose green and purple as the colors. That's just hideous. Kind of scary actually."

Bounce smirked and smacked Evan's head as he walked past, grumbling, "It's her favorite colors. Don't even ask."

CHAPTER EIGHTEEN

Pawn

Lucifer loved a good party, but the wedding of his brother to a human wasn't his idea of a party. What god or immortal would marry a frail, delicate mortal being? He had not been invited—no surprise really. Bounce did not consider him a friend and he was pretty sure completely detested him. They kept their dealings with obtaining new coming arrivals in Hell on a business level. Whatever. He also knew that part of the reason for that detachment is he had refused to ever explain why he had once called Bounce brother; even now he would not explain. Bounce had finally stopped asking, but the resentment ran deep.

So, as he stood hidden in shadow on the second story balcony looking down at the festivities below, he felt a twinge of happiness for Bounce and that was the real reason he was here. To see joy on a face that had once looked at him in kindness and friendship, as he only wanted what was best for one who had been through so much. Remembered or not.

As he stood there, he felt a power, trying to hide as well, appear on the second story. Looking left, he saw none other than the beautiful Lachesis, goddess of fate. That was surprising, but when given some thought, perhaps not. As far as he had observed, she had listened when she was told to stay away from Bounce and the fact that she was masking her presence made him believe she had no plans to interrupt the happy occasion.

"What a sad pair we are, yes?" He said the words so only she could hear them in her mind. She looked over at him, shocked to see him there, so absorbed in watching Bounce below as he joked with his wedding party.

She covered that shock quickly but not quickly enough... she didn't know Bounce was getting married. That fact was plain and simple in her mind. A mind that was scrambling to deal with her love going to another. So, if she didn't know that, Lucifer thought, why was she here?

Bounce was getting married. Lachesis had no idea how she felt about that but it was making her heart ache as she watched him below. He looked happier than she had ever seen him and she had to wipe tears from her eyes to see him so.

Until Lucifer made his presence known that is. She sent him a glare as she straightened her back to lift her chin. "We are indeed sad." She glanced at him and raked her eyes over him, as she gave a dry smile. "So, I assume you didn't get an invite. That's terrible. Poor," emphasizing the final word with a smirk, "thing."

He laughed at her snideness as he came to stand next to her, both of them hidden from the others at will. "I see you didn't get an invite either. But you didn't know about our mutual love getting married, now did you?" He turned to rest an elbow on the rail, tilting his head to regard her. "So, I must ask myself, why are you here? And why are you hiding?"

"None of your business, Devil." She moved away from him, glancing upstairs to Bounce's loft and back. "But I am not here for the wedding and you're wrong if you think I'm not happy about it. I love that he is happy." She glanced at him once more. "As I am sure you are."

He snorted and braced his hands on the rail to watch below when he saw it. A child?

The Fate had thought, for the briefest moment, how a child was why she was here. It was the key to all

Bounce needed?

What?

He narrowed his gaze as he regarded her and then it hit him. She had hid all that she had learned from Bounce's thread that he was sure of. Otherwise the other Fates and Gods would have used that. He always wondered where and then as he walked away from her to cast his eyes to the top story, he sensed not one, but two lives there.

Tricky, tricky fate Bitch.

She had hidden Bounce's thread, with all it contained—the man's past, whom and what he was, and most of all, Lucifer's own betrayal of his brother—within the thread of a child not yet born. Fear and sorrow washed through him as he realized the brilliance of such a plan. He would have admired the Fate if it didn't mean destroying the deals he had made for Bounce's safety. And his own. And for mankind to survive. He closed his eyes as he listened to Bounce's booming sounds of laughter below, sharing toasts with the wedding party as they waited for his lovely bride to join him.

Turning away from the fate, who was so attentive to watching below, he made his way up the stairs towards the third floor, pausing for the briefest of seconds to curl his hand into a fist. A portal straight from Hell opened in the basement below the club, filling the space with Eaters, the primary foe in the war. "I'm sorry brother," as he continued up the stairs.

"Boss!" The yell had Bounce spinning around as the doors from the basement burst open, Eaters slithering and snarling as they burst into the club. Some were in human form whereas others had not bothered to take on that deception.

"Breakers! Get the humans clear!" Bounce yelled as he caught the two twin 9mm's Evan threw him from behind the bar. Several Breakers broke off to corral the humans not trained to fight behind it, and then jumping up on it to defend them. The Relays that could fight were unsheathing blades, pulling guns from holsters. The Eaters attacking now was second thought to destroying the invasion before it got to the streets outside. Bounce fired his guns, glancing upstairs, waving a hand to lock his loft door from the outside to keep Tanya inside and safe. Never was he so glad he had it reinforced and sound proofed than he was at that moment. He then turned his full attention with a battle cry to ridding the celebration of the nasty, ugly gate crashers.

Lucifer walked down the private hall, passing through the velvet rope with its signage that said "Private - No Admittance" as if it wasn't there. Dropping his hand to his side, he flexed his fingers to manifest a Reaper Blade. Curved and deadly like a small scythe, the blade was black Damascus steel and the handle polished rosewood. He flexed his fingers around the handle as he came to stand in front of Bounce's private loft, sensing the lockdown the god had put on it. Shame it didn't stop him as he appeared on the other side, the lock remaining in place, never touched.

Bounce's lovely bride was humming in front of a full-length mirror, her belly extended with child as she straightened dark purple and greenery which was formed into a crown on her head. Her soft brown hair was pulled up, but sweetly leaving some to frame her pretty face. She turned to join her husband to be and that's when she saw him.

"Oh." She gave a nervous smile as she looked behind him, expecting someone else and then back. "Did they send you up to get me? Bounce is so silly, doesn't like me going up the stairs by myself being this preggo. It's sweet. I'm really clumsy like this." Her smile wavered as she took a step back. "Are you a friend of his?"

Lucifer smiled, hiding the weapon behind his long, red leather coat as he stepped forward. "I am. And you look beautiful. I can see why he loves you so. And you bear his child." His eyes went down to her belly as flames started licking in the blue of them, before he lifted them to hers. "He must be so happy. As are you, yes?" He took another step until he was standing right in front of her. "Tell me sweet Tanya, did Bounce make you happy and feel loved?" He tilted her chin up to look into his eyes. The moment her brown ones met his, he could see her becoming mesmerized, like prey in the aim of a serpent's strike.

She whispered, her eyes becoming glazed, "Yes. He made me happy. And loved." A soft whimper touched her voice, her mind trying to regain control in the alarm of danger as she whispered, "You're not his friend. Are you?"

He smiled, his lips spreading over his fangs, exposing their length and sharpness. "Oh my dear. But I am. More than he will ever know."

"Check the damn basement. I want it sealed and make sure none of these bitches remain alive." He wiped Eater fluid from his cheek as he looked around the club, kicking an Eater body as it was already turning into watery slime. The table of food had been knocked over and blood and gore from the demons splattered the walls and pooled on the floor. It made no sense.

Eaters didn't survive long on the Earth plane when they weren't fully formed into that of a human after taking their spark. Why they called them Eaters—they could use a human's spark to appear like the one whose spark they had devoured, even use their memories to masquerade as them, but without that spark, they couldn't survive here very long, their sparks were just leftover junk when they were made. So why would unlit Eaters bother coming here?

He'd have to figure it out later as he started to bark orders for both securing the club and getting it cleaned up. Nothing, not even the damn war, was going to stop him from marrying Tanya today.

As his eyes went upward, they stopped on the second floor, not sure if what he was seeing was actually there. But then she gave a smile as he whispered, "Nani?"

Tanya couldn't help the tears that flowed from her eyes, though for some reason she couldn't seem to move and speaking was a struggle as she seemed pinned by the gaze of this being that held her with his eyes. She let out a soft sob, whispering with her voice shaking, "Please. He loves me. We're getting married. We're having a child. Please."

Lucifer tilted his head, giving her a sad look as he sighed. Placing his lips against her forehead, he whispered against her warm skin, "I know. And that, I can't allow."

The blade struck fast and he stepped back as blood and water from her womb splashed on the floor, onto his blood red leather boots, turning them black. His hold on her mind released as he moved away, causing her to stumble back, clutching her belly. She looked down as she bled before looking back up at him, crying in pain, "Why?!"

He brought the blade up to lick the fluid from it as he met her eyes over it. "It's simple. It has nothing to do with you. Or that child. You two are simply pawns. But, it's not time for this game to end. It doesn't end until I want it to."

Lachesis didn't mean for Bounce to see her, but her will to be unseen had slipped when she got caught up in the battle below. As he came up the stairs, she took a deep breath to settle herself, to try to think straight before he arrived. She should have known it was useless as he walked up and swept her up into a hug. A hug she had not expected.

"You don't hate me?"

He stood back to look down at her, a frown appearing on his brow. "Why would I hate you? I know you tried to save me that day. And I know you had no choice to leave me in Hell." He cupped her face and said softly, "I could never hate you, Nani. And that anger was put away long ago. I have thought of you many times. But," the frown deepened as he looked downward, "your timing isn't the best." He let out a soft chuckle. "It's my wedding day."

Lachesis placed her palms on that strong chest, looking up at him with a teary smile. "I know. And she's having your child. There's something very important I need to tell you."

"Bounce?"

He almost didn't hear his bride as he looked over his shoulder, her voice so weak and small. "Tanya?" He rushed to catch her as she crumbled towards the floor. He landed on his knees, his eyes wide with alarm as he looked at all the blood, clutching her close to him in his arms. "Tanya? Oh god, what happened? Tanya!"

Tanya looked up at him, her hand coming up to press against his cheek, her fingers so pale and cold. "I love you. I love you so much. I wanted to marry you so bad. To see our baby. I wonder if she would have," her eyes fluttering closed, her words falling away, "had your beautiful eyes..."

Bounce felt the hot tears sting as he looked down at her, Breakers running to get the healers from the bottom floor, screams as more joined them upstairs. But all that faded away as he held the woman he loved, the mother of his child—they were fading too.

He pressed his hand over her stomach, trying to feel the light that was there just hours ago. But there was so much blood and he tried not to look or feel the horrific slash that went from her waist to breast. He held her tight, meeting her eyes, watching them close as he cried out, his voice a desperate roar, "You will marry me! You will have our child! Do you hear me, Tanya! God damn it! Do not close your eyes! Do you hear me?!"

But he knew she was gone for he felt both her light and that of their child's grow dim and then dark as if it had been fused to his. He put back his head and roared in pain, as everyone else stood in sorrow around him. He barely sensed Linda Devenmore gently checking for signs of life of both his love and his child, shaking her head as she cried, saying softly they were gone. He wasn't even aware when Tanya's body was removed from his arms, or everyone trying to reach his mind—a mind that was shattering under the overwhelming weight of grief and loss. He couldn't have told who touched him, who offered comfort or how he had found his way to a chair.

All he knew was that he felt like he was falling. Falling painfully and fast. And he prayed, wished and begged... *Please... don't let me survive this fall.*

THE AFTERMATH

A Deal

Lucifer found him in the locked, dark club, hours later. Bounce had thrown everyone else out, some he had hit and battered to go. Now, the god sat on the club's bar, his bride to be laid beside him on the glass surface, quiet and pale in death. Bounce himself look dead, not moving and so still Lucifer wasn't sure the man actually did still live.

He walked behind the bar and pulled up a bottle of whiskey, finding two glasses and poured them both one, his eyes lifting to Bounce, who had still not moved. Walking to stand in front of him, he held out the glass to say softly, "Drink." When Bounce didn't move, he sat it next to him.

Bounce lifted his eyes to Lucifer's, a scowl touching his lips as his eyes phased to a deep red. "You've said that before. And look where it's gotten me."

Lucifer smirked as he downed the whiskey, rolling the glass in his fingers. "It saved your life. You're welcome." He reached past him to get the bottle, pausing to look at the dead woman and grimace. "That's not the best décor for the club. Surely, there's some ritual you need to do, yes?"

Bounce was on him fast, grabbing his black coat to slam the devil against the wall, his fangs bared under curled lips. "I'm done. You hear me? I'm done!"

Lucifer raised a brow and lifted the bottle to his lips, taking a deep drink as he looked at Bounce. "Done? I don't think so." He shoved Bounce off of him and walked around him to kick a chair upright, sitting on it backwards, wrapping his arms around the top. "Because I believe there is more that you want. And I'll give it to you if, like I said before, you lead this war and end it for the good of mankind." He took another drink and held the bottle out. "Here. Let's drink on it."

Bounce let out a snarl, knocking the bottle from Lucifer's hand to send it shattering on the far wall. Grabbing his coat once again, he hauled him up and got in his face. "No. Nothing you can promise me can make me fight. Not any longer. Nothing. It took away what meant the most to me. Nothing! Nothing you offer can fix that. Can make it not hurt. To make me not want to die just to be with them!"

He let him go and kicked the chair so Lucifer wouldn't even have that, turning his back to the being, hoping that he would do the deed. "I'm leaving. Never to be seen again. I'll live in solitude, away from the war. Away from all the pain it brings. Away from all the pain I seem to bring to anyone that cares about me. I'll never love again. It's toxic."

Lucifer had predicted this and straightened up his jacket, rolling his head on his neck. Lying was a talent, and it was one that the devil was the best at. If doing so got them both where they needed to be on the path of destiny, then so be it. "I think you're wrong."

Bounce let out another snarl and whipped around prepared to rip the devil's head off and froze. "What is that?"

Lucifer had his palm held up, and above it two swirling bright sparks spun, twisting on each other as if one. But two very separate lights. Lucifer smiled and said softly, following Bounce's amazing gaze, "I rescued them. Kept them from going to hell with the Eater that killed them. I thought, perhaps, it would be something you want. I knew you wouldn't want them to burn in Hell."

Emotions overwhelmed Bounce, sending him crashing to his knees as his eyes, turning a stormy dark grey, locked on the brilliant light that was held suspended above Lucifer's palm. "Tanya? Our baby?"

Lucifer went to his haunches, and said softly, "Yes. And I will give them to you, so that you and they can live in eternity. But there's a price."

Bounce couldn't take his eyes off the light as he nodded his head, hand reaching out to feel the warmth of those he loved, his beautiful face looking worn and pained. "Anything. Whatever you want, don't let them go to hell." His eyes then went to Lucifer's as he pleaded, his voice cracking in pain, "They're pure. Good and light. Please, I'll do anything not to have them go there."

Lucifer smiled, the light of the sparks of Bounce's heart lighting up his features in an eerie glow. "Then fight the war. Lead it to victory. Save mankind and I promise you, the high place in Heaven will be given to you and those you love. It's that simple."

Bounce frowned as his mind tried to fire on all cylinders and failing, gaze going back to the sparks. "And until then? You'll keep them safe?"

"I swear on every drop of blood I have. That within me and within you. They will be suspended and the time just a blink for them until you are together again." He stood and looked down at Bounce, holding out his other hand. "Do you wish to make the deal?"

Bounce closed his eyes as he rose to his feet. "Yes." He clasped his hand with the devil's and the sighed as the sparks vanished. "Do not trick me, Devil. And you better carry out our deal, or so help me," lifting his eyes to Lucifer's, "I'll gut you and feed your own entrails to your demons and let you watch."

Lucifer gave a smile and shrugged. "I might enjoy that." He let go of Bounce's hand and then said softly, eyes going to the dead woman, "I am sorry for your loss. There is nothing like losing someone you love." He swung his suddenly sorrow-filled gaze to Bounce. "It never stops hurting, Brother."

Bounce turned away from him, walking over to pick Tanya up in his arms before giving Lucifer a dark glare. "Do not call me that. I'm not your brother." He then carried off the only woman he loved, leaving Lucifer standing, as he often was, alone.

Lucifer blew out a breath as he watched him go, turning to leave himself and said softly.

"But that's what you are, Gabriel."

THE END...

OF BOUNCE'S STORY

SO FAR.

SNEAK PEEK AT BOOK FOUR IN THE GRID SERIES:

LUST

Available Now!

CHAPTER ONE

"I don't think this is very smart Reno." He glanced at Bella with a grin. "Neither do I. But it's all we got. And hey! That's something right?" He gave her wide fanged smile and two thumbs up. Bella just stared at him, muttering out "unbelievable", before she tapped in her code to the keypad by the back door of the heart of the Grid station. He wiggled his fingers to help with his nerves as the door popped open. Bella entered and he was right behind her. His eyes went up to see a security camera swivel their way and he threw his hand out. Wisps swarmed and coated the lens seconds before its electronic eye landed on them. Bella froze in her tracks at the sight and blew out an awed, "Whoa. That is so cool."

Reno chuckled as he passed the young Rely with his senses alert to the open space in front of them saying low, "You think that's cool? Just wait, I got all kinds of stuff." He turned his head to wink at her as he headed down the hall.

Witch had wanted him to at least bring a gun, a dagger, something—but he didn't want to be a threat. He just needed to see the dead woman who had come back to life. Alive, but different. Just like he did three months ago after being slaughtered ruthlessly by a man he found out later was his father. Sorta. Well, asshole had been the sire of this body, not him. No, he was a whole different thing all together—the body was just the latest feature.

Reno Sundown was what he now knew as—A Shadow-Keeper. Called a Keeper, he was now a being created to harness and maintain one of the darkest powers of mankind; feeding it but never letting it get out of control to destroy the human world. But the greed of the god that made him, which coincidentally was also Epsilon, the father of this body, had gotten in the way and his creation had been screwed up. Reno had instead manifested as the dark-side of hero's personality by the name of Jess Bailey, who was a Breaker. Breakers were immortal bad-asses on the Grid that protected mankind by keeping dark from devouring every soul on the planet. All of which were connected and monitored until mankind could protect itself and darkness chased from the world.

Reno used to be a Breaker when he was first removed from Jess' mind and given—tada—this body. But it had its issues too—like now having a split personality of his very own, a dark side named Sundown. But they worked pretty well together in the new body and their new life was getting better by the day. Until Reno got slaughtered and his Keeper purpose was then able to take over his true reason for being with nothing in the way.

For all the Grid knew? He was still dead and his body was never found. And it had been that way for months as he learned his new powers and skills. One of the things he had to learn to deal with was his blood was no longer blood, but literally a portion of the power he kept. Insanity, going by the title of Madness, whose color of choice apparently was black so, that was the color of Reno's blood. He had no heartbeat or body heat. And since he was really just an upper-class animated corpse (he hated the word zombie) he was already dead. Keepers couldn't really die again; they just went to a place between realms called the Void. The same place the powers were kept. As long as a Keeper didn't have their head severed from their spine or bleed out, their powers made sure they made it back to their bodies. It didn't usually take long, for they healed really fast too.

As cool as that sounded, however, there is always a price and the same applied to the Void. It always took something for hosting you and your power to send you back to the world of the living. Memories. Skills or other important thing you might need. There was no way of knowing. Reno was kind of avoiding the Void for those very reasons alone. He was pretty much flawed as hell already so the thought of losing the ability to pee standing up or something was scary. But even worse, forgetting the woman he loved or her child he had come to adore. Nope. Not going to the Void anytime soon.

Until tonight he and the woman Emma, who he called Witch, were the only ones that knew he existed after being declared dead. That was until Bella, a young Tech Relay on the Grid, had walked in on them doing well, uh, naughty things. She had been staying with Witch to help with her daughter, Sophia. Who, he called Rugrat (yeah, he had nicknames for a lot of people). After the shock and her almost shooting him as he stood there naked wore off, she had told him about a woman brought in for lockdown at the Grid. A woman who they had found slaughtered.

And had come back. But different, just like him.

He needed to see that woman. They thought he was the only Keeper and he was definitely the first one, albeit he got a little lost for over a century, but maybe this woman was another of his kind and he had to know.

"Freeze! Hands over your head."

Reno's eyes drifted over to Bella's with a wince as he did as they were told. "Oops. Yep, bad idea."

CHAPTER TWO

"**B**oss! You need to get out here. Now!' The alert through his stamp in the form of a loud yelling Relay in his head was not the thing the god Bounce wanted to hear in the morning—especially before he even finished his first cup of coffee. He sighed and grumbled back to the integrated link via the Grid, "What is it? I'm cranky."

"Reno's alive. And boss? He's here."

That had the almost seven-foot tall god on his feet, coffee forgotten, and running to the main operations center of the Grid station. This has got to be a joke, he thought as he ran. Reno had been killed more than three months ago and his body found after a very fucked up few weeks. Then...that same body had been taken right out from under their noses in the middle of the night by the goddess Yin Yang. That's when he had found out the body used to make Reno had been Epsilon's son, and Epsilon was the one and only sick offspring of Lucifer. But why Yin took Reno's remains he wasn't able to get out of the goddess of balance—the bitch just enjoyed her games way too much.

As he ran, he commanded to control, "I want all guns hot and trained on Reno. Do not let that man move without a bullet ready to stop him, do you get my drift?" The voice that came back through the mental link said a curt, "Yes Sir". He hit the command center and slid to a stop on his high top sneakers to see that Reno was indeed standing there, along with the young Relay Bella, kept behind the man. A dozen or so Recons along with Breakers had surrounded him with guns held at the ready, safeties off. Narrowing his eyes, Bounce walked to the edge of the circle to scrutinize the "dead man".

He was pale yet there was an energy vibrating from him. Reno's eyes were always a brilliant blue but now they seemed even more so. But the man's chest rose and fell as well as hands flexed at his side as if trying to stay calm. But Bounce could tell this wasn't the same Reno they had seen before who was falling apart before he died—there was something more intense, more predator like. And more importantly? Bounce didn't detect even a hint of life in the man as he said low, 'You're dead."

Reno smiled, just as easy and goofy as before, turning his gaze to Bounce. "Yep. Totally. Hi Bounce."

A Tech Relay stepped up to Bounce and whispered in amazement, swallowing down just to be able to speak, "He's saying the truth Boss. No heartbeat and no heat signature. He's dead. I've never seen anything like him." The Relay backed away to whisper, "And he's got dark energy, just like the woman."

It wasn't the first time Reno had guns pointed at him. Shoot, as the split personality of a gun-slinging outlaw, it used to be an almost daily occurrence. But he really should have thought this through. Things like what to say when they realized he was dead would have been a good idea. Oh and when he was asked what he was, which he was sure was happening any minute, how to explain just what he was. Yeah, he was the worse at making decisions and this instance was just another indicator of that.

His gaze scanned the men and women with guns pointed at his head and heart to determine distance, speed and how much damage could be done and not done. Already Sundown, his dark side was gearing up to send a jolt of adrenaline and power to carry out any action they needed to survive. Well, survive as much as a dead guy could survive—gosh it got confusing sometimes. Witch would so be saying, "I told you so" when and if he got out of this without going to the Void.

"I need to see that woman Bounce. I came unarmed and don't want to have to get messy, but I need to see her."

Bounce snorted as he walked through the armed personnel to look down at Reno at a distance of about six-feet away. "So, you've been dead. Still are dead, come in here without a heads up", nailed his eyes to Bella who shrunk farther behind Reno, "and I'm supposed to just say sure, come in Reno. Want some cookies and milk?" He crossed his arms on his huge chest with a smirk, voice full of authority, "Not happening. Not until you explain how you're here and what you are."

Reno's gaze swung back to Bounce's with nod. "Okay. You and me talk", waved a hand around at the others, "alone and without enough beads on my brain to make a necklace."

Bounce gave a nod and held his hand out towards his office, letting Reno lead the way. Paused and pointed to Bella, barking out, "Secure her until you hear from me. But non-hostile handling. In other words", turned to follow Reno, "don't hurt her. Yet."

"So explain."

Reno looked around Bounce's office and noticed the god hadn't even repaired the dent in the wall left from the last time they "talked". Sat down in front of the desk and shrugged. "Uh. I was dead, then Yin Yang and Omega brought me back. Seems like I'm a Shadow-Keeper. Been lost like a long time. So, once I was dead that purpose could take over and I'm back to serve my dark power." He smiled. "Insanity if you can believe that one. Goes by the name of Madness. It's kinda fun and entertaining."

Bounce gave him an incredulous glance as he too sat down to face Reno from behind the desk. "You're the lost Keeper? I thought that was just myth. An urban legend..." He sat back and carefully picked up the Rubik's Cube from its stand to roll it in his hands, ensuring he didn't change the order of the colored squares. "So Yin figured it out and got the Omega to give you a spark? Your new purpose?" His brows went down. "Well, your original purpose. That's a messed up story right out of Final Fantasy, you are aware of that right?"

Reno laughed and ran a hand through his hair. "Oh I totally know it's messed up. But it's the truth." He stood up to brace his arms on Bounce's desk. "Bella told me about the woman you found. How she was slaughtered and then came back alive. Let me guess—no heartbeat, no body temperature and her blood is black right?"

Bounce sat back and shook his head. "Two out of three isn't bad."

Reno frowned as his eyes slid left then right in thought before going back to meet Bounce's eyes. "Wait, which two did I get right?"

Bounce stood. "Her blood is purple. Same as her eyes. Come with me."

CHAPTER THREE

McKenzie Miller had no idea how long she had screamed. Kenzie Miller was not a screamer—until now. Just that it hurt like nothing she had ever imagined; and considering her fucked up life, that imagination didn't have to be too huge. Her body felt like it was being ripped apart from the inside with her head being the ground zero of that agony. Now hours, days, hell maybe weeks later, her throat felt the brunt of that pain in the fact her screams came out in a hoarse croaking sound without much volume. She sat curled up in the corner of a padded room, her hospital gown soaked in sweat with her hair a matted mess from the same.

She had no idea where she was or who these people were that gawked at her through what she somehow sensed was a two-way mirror. She sensed them. She knew as much as she could count her fingers that there were four people standing on the other side of that glazed silver surface and all of them were whispering about her. Staring at her as if she was the freakiest goldfish in the world. She glared at the glass and brought up her hands, both of them shaking to flip them off, a weak smile crossing her lips.

"There she is. No one can go in there with her. She freaks out more and they do as well. So we have her isolated." Bounce looked over at Reno and back to watch the girl, his voice failing to sound detached, "Whatever she's going through must hurt like a bitch. She's screamed from the moment she came back from the dead."

Reno leaned forward to look at the woman and felt sorry for her immediately. "It hurts like crazy and I was a Breaker." He glanced at Bounce. "Was she human before? What do we know?"

Bounce turned to rest against the counter of monitors and devices and lifted his shoulders as he crossed his arms. "Yes. Totally human but any other details? Nothing. We can't get her to tell us her name. And we ran her through facial recognition and it got no returns. So either she's been a good little human with no run-ins with the law or her record is sealed. With that being said, no, we don't know shit about our screaming mimi in there." Bounce lowered his head as his brow came down to say low so the other three men couldn't hear, "We do know she was raped repeatedly and then stabbed several times. The last blow sliced her heart in two."

Reno's head twisted fast to look at Bounce after those statements, with a sinking ball of dread twisting in his gut. "Raped? And her heart was sliced in two?" Epsilon. Had to be. And judging by Bounce's face, the god knew it too. Epsilon had done the same death blow to the heart when he had been killed. He stood and blew out a breath. "I need to see her. Now."

Bounce reached over to place his hand on Reno's chest and yanked it away fast. "Damn. You are cold." He turned to face him as he rested a hip. "No. Can't allow it. I know you're being honest with me. But I also don't know all the facts of how or why you're back. Nor do I get the darkness we're picking up off of you. It's the same," threw a thumb pointed back behind him at the woman, "type of power we feel off of her. But we know that when she freaks? It drains the Grid and we can't allow that. The two of you together? No. Not happening."

Reno rubbed a hand over his face and shook his head. "I need to see her Bounce. I can help her. If she's like me she's scared and confused. I can get her past that." He glanced over at the god with his fangs bared as his jaw tightened. "You can't keep her locked up like this. That's torture in itself."

Bounce looked back at the woman and without even batting an eye, stated as simple as if he wanted to go for drive for ice cream. "You're right. It is. It's why we have slated to destroy her in forty-eight hours. Can't take the chance of a hit to the Grid from a being like that getting loose." He looked at Reno. "So you don't have to worry. Besides, she was dead already."

Reno gawked and before he knew it, he had grabbed Bounce until the god's back met the wall. The four men in the room jumped up, pulling out guns to aim. He spun and put the god between them as he snarled out, "You know, you tried that bit with me. Destroying me? It didn't work out too well." He peeked over the god's shoulder at the four men and back to Bounce. "And I can take them out. You too. I am not the same joke I was before." One of the men made a move and suddenly wisps whipped out from their Keeper and swarmed the man. The Relay backed up with a scream as the tiny being's nipped and hissed at him, the gun clattering to the floor. "Now. Can we discuss a second option? Or do I show you just how much I've changed?"

Bounce raised a brow at the wisps and nodded, as he shoved Reno away from him. "No need. And you do that to me again?" He pointed a finger in Reno's face. "You'll get to see how far I'm willing to go to not let you."

"They should be back by now," Emma Devenmore pulled yet another tray of cookies from the oven. Turning, she realized she had run out of spots in which to cool the latest batch. Fine, so she had a habit of baking when she was stressed and worried. "Good thing Candyman loves my cookies." It was true—Reno loved eating sweets but not only that, the sugar helped keep his head quiet when both his dark side, Sundown and Madness were wanting attention. It was for the same reason he had earned the nick-name Candyman—Reno always had candy on him, his confection of choice being Twizzlers. The man seemed to constantly have one spinning around his tongue or close at hand.

She had walked into dining room and sat the sheet of cookies there on the table when she heard the sounds of car doors from the driveway behind the house. Tossing her oven mitt, she ran to the back door and threw it open, relief washing over her when she saw Reno and Bella walking up to the house. Running, she threw herself in Reno's arms, wrapping her arms and legs around him to bury her face against his neck. She smiled when she felt the warmth flush his skin from his heart beating at her touch—a heart that only beat for her. She moved her head to meet his eyes as he continued to walk towards the house. "So you don't seem to have any new holes. It went well?"

They reached the house and he let her slide down to stand. "Well, if you consider a bunch of guns wanting to shoot me. Bounce threatening to do bad things to the dead guy you love? Sure. Went just great!" He smiled as he bent his head to kiss her, loving how each touch and kiss of his Witch made him come alive—literally. It was her touch, and only her touch that made that dead heart inside of his chest and the black fluid of his power pulse like blood, warming his skin and giving the feeling of being alive. He loved it—but not as much as he loved her.

"Oh! Is that fresh cookies?"

Bella pushed by them and he looked down at Emma to say with a whine, "She's going to eat all those cookies."

Emma laughed as she splayed her hands on his chest. "There is no chance of that. Trust me." She took his hand in hers and pulled him over to the breakfast bar to sit, handing him a plate of warm cookies. "So what happened? What did Bounce say? Did you see the woman?"

He took a few cookies, eyes rolling in pleasure at the taste of them as he shoved them in his mouth, talking around them. "They freaked. Still freaked to see I'm alive, well, dead alive. Bounce knew about the Keeper legend so that helped. I saw the woman through glass because they have her locked up. And she looks bad Witch, real bad."

Bella came over to sit with them, bringing all three of them a glass of milk and nodded as she listened. "They said they found her out at the old Presidio Hospital. A Muni found her. She had been bound, gagged and they said all kinds of stuff had been done to her. But I do know they said she had been dead for more than a day or so. All stiff and everything."

Reno glanced over at Witch as he dunked a cookie in the milk, deciding not to discuss the most horrific details of the woman's condition in front of the seventeen-year old Relay. "She apparently came to, back alive, whatever, while she was still in the body bag as they were heading back to the base. She went nuts and made the two Muni's run off the road scared as heck. I can guess that would freak just about anyone out. But they got her back to the Grid, tried to clean her up and put her in a padded room. No one can get close."

Bella finished her cookies and milk. "I'm going to check out my Facebook." She snagged a few cookies to take with her and left the two of them alone.

As soon as she went to her room, Reno sat his cookie down and turned to face Witch, his voice sad and soft, "She was raped. Several times they said. And stabbed..." reached over to take her hand, knowing the next part might bring back memories of when she had to prepare his body when he was killed, "with her heart sliced in two."

Witch's eyes widened as her hand tightened on his. "Do you think it was Epsilon? Why would he do that?" Reno blew out a long, frustrated breath as he leaned over to put his forehead on her shoulder. "Because he's trying to make more Keepers and he's trying to have control."

Emma brought a hand up to sink in his soft hair, stroking her fingers through the wavy locks that never seemed to want to behave. "We need to help her Reno. We have to. We can't let him get to her."

He nodded, sighing in pleasure at her touch against his scalp. "We are. But you may not like how I have to do it."

THE GRID GLOSSARY

There are many types of beings on the Grid. Here are just a few:

Breakers: Supernatural heroes with a dark past. For the price a coin containing their soul, they are bought from Hell by Bounce to become part of the Grid where they fight the darkness and destroy the demons from Hell, called Eaters. If they do their job well, when the war ends, or they find love, they get a second chance at life if found worthy and obtain both freedom and immortality for themselves and those they love.

Relays: Human and other counterparts of the Grid. There are several kinds just as with any army.

Tech Relays: The computer and technical side of the Grid. They monitor and maintain the vast Grid located in Fort Pearce under the Golden Gate Bridge. Techs have limited fighting skills but incredible analytical abilities.

Recon Relays: The human counterparts who are trained to have both fighting and tactical skills as well as trained as snipers. Recon Relays are the ones who hunt down those wishing to destroy or harm the Grid on the inside.

Wires: The top of the human Recon food chain, these human counterparts go through an intense testing process to prove they are the best of all the humans that fight on the Grid.

 **Healer Relays:** Humans and deities who serve to heal those on the Grid. Gifted with the talent of touch-electrotherapy, they can access their spark to heal another. If they tap too much, their spark goes dark, and they die.

 **Bridge Relays:** The engineers of the Grid who not only worked closely with Tesla in its design but are constantly designing new technology to ensure it stays ahead of the war and to assist those on the Grid.

 **Municipal (Muni) Relays:** These are humans who work for the various branches of government and agencies in the city. They are aware of the Grid and use their positions to keep it hidden. Some examples include deputy mayor, police officers, and firemen.

 **Other Designation:** This designation is for other beings on The Grid with no standard classification.

 **Vampire:** Not part of the Grid but working closely with Bounce and the High Council to   align the two races and armies. Based in New Orleans.

Shadow-Keepers:

Known as Keepers, they are at the top of the food chain on the Grid. These beings are animated by the dark power that must exist to keep the balance of dark and light. The Keepers walk the shadow in between by feeding their powers while keeping them controlled so the darkness never overcomes and destroys the light.

Reno Sundown: Keeper of Madness and former Breaker on the Grid. The first Keeper created by Epsilon, son of Lucifer.

Make sure you join the reader and character interaction group on Facebook. Not only can you chat with Ward, but you can also discuss with some of the characters you met in this book!

Yes, even Reno.

Join it here:

http://bit.ly/GridNightsFandom

And if you want to dive into another Ward World, check out her Soul Bound Trilogy.

You can find Book I: The Warrior here –

https://books2read.com/SoulBoundOne

Be warned, you may not survive the read.

#SBSurviveTheRead

Join Ward's Newsletter here for exclusive FIRST LOOKS & Other Member Exclusive Content:

www.AuthorJasTWard.com

ALSO WRITTEN BY JAS T. WARD

Poetry & Short Stories
Bits & Pieces

Dark Paranormal Romance

The Grid Series
Reading Order
Candyman: Book One
Madness: Book Two
Bounce: Book Three
Lust: Book Four
Cowboy: Book Five
Murder: Book Six
Envy: Book Seven
Hostage: Spin-Off*
Chaos: Book Eight
Sundown: The Final

** K. Bromberg's*
Everyday Heroes World

The Soul Bound Trilogy
Reading Order
The Warrior: Book One
The Wounded: Book Two
The Wanted: Book Three

Contemporary Romance (Standalones)
A Little Pill Called Love
Love's Bitter Harvest

ABOUT THE AUTHOR

"I am the product of several realities making the whole: a troubled childhood, domestic violence survivor, homeless person, single mother and a murder/suicide survivor. But in every single one of those realities, one thing remained true - my imagination."
Reading and writing has always been Ms. Ward's escape. And she wants to continue to give that to her readers as well. Known for action, drama, laughter, darkness and twists you don't see coming in the same book, Ward is known for writing books that are diverse, different and unique. A bestselling author on both Amazon and ARe Romance, Ms. Ward's books have won awards from various blogs and Preditors and Editors in the categories of reader favorites, best dark romance and others. Ms. Ward's books have also been reviewed in Ind'Tale Magazine and been nominated for their prestigious RONE awards for each time a finalist.
Born and raised in Texas and spending time living in Kentucky, Ms. Ward spends her days and nights writing as therapy to deal with life and all that it brings—from the past and present. And hopefully finds joy, laughter and fun to mix in with the dark. Something her readers have come to love in her works. She is the proud parent of three very independent grown children and grandmother to three delightful grandchildren. She has two fur babies that sit and ponder why their human is talking to herself late into the night as she writes out colorful and diverse if not twisted characters and tales.
Links so we can keep in touch.

Website: www.AuthorJasTWard.com
You can sign up for my newsletter and get a free read!

9 781637 325957